TOUCH OF DARKNESS
MAGIC, NEW MEXICO

⚜

ML GUIDA

BOOK 7

Copyright © 2018 by ML Guida

All rights reserved.

No part of this book may be reproduced in any form or by any electronic or mechanical means, including information storage and retrieval systems, without written permission from the author, except for the use of brief quotations in a book review.

The author of this Book has been granted permission by S.E. Smith to use the copyrighted characters and/or worlds created by S.E. Smith in this book; all copyright protection to the characters and/or worlds of Magic, New Mexico are retained by S.E. Smith

This book was originally a kindle world book and it was part of S.E. Smith's Magic, New Mexico.

❦ Created with Vellum

FOREWORD

Imagine The Worlds of Magic, New Mexico... A series that brings together outstanding paranormal and science fiction authors to expand a town where witches, aliens, vampires, werewolves, goblins, sorceresses, pirates, time travelers, and paranormal live in harmony - when they aren't joining forces to defeat the bad guys. A magical town where being abnormal is the norm!

I'm S.E. Smith, the creator of Magic, New Mexico and I invite you to curl up with each book now and discover all the action, the magic, and the love that makes Magic, New Mexico the ultimate go-to series for Paranormal / Science Fiction Romance readers.

For all the stories, go to MagicNewMexico.com/books/. Grab your copy today!

CHAPTER 1

"You're dying. The cancer has gone into your bone marrow." Dr. Havens sat on his stool, then shut his chart like a prison door.

Donald Elliott rubbed his sweating forehead and struggled to breathe, the antiseptic stench nearly choking him. The paper gown stuck to his slick skin. "Are you sure? The treatments, the medications…"

Dr. Havens shook his head. His thick spiky gray hair made him look like a mad scientist. "I'm sorry, Donald, but they're not working."

Donald's heart beat harder and blood pumped through him. Heat rushed over his face. He threw up his hands. "That's it. I die? I'm only twenty-six years old." He broke out into a loud hacking, his lungs rattling. God, he was so tired of it. He should be out playing football or shooting golf like he had in high school–not holed up in his house sweating and losing weight as if he were anorexic.

"I know." The doctor's voice thickened, and he hung his head. "But there are very little treatments for stage IV Non-Hodgkins Lymphoma. If only we would have discovered it sooner."

"So, then what do I do now? Curl up and wait to die?" Bitterness swirled in his gut.

"I can refer you to the Cancer Treatment Center in New Mexico. They've had good luck in treating Non-Hodgkins."

Donald ripped off his gown and reached for his suit. "I thought you were supposed to be the best. I spent enough money here, doing all your damn experiments."

Dr. Havens straightened and pushed his wire glasses back on his beak nose. "I *am* the best. My team and I have done everything we can."

Donald gritted his teeth. "Your best hasn't been good enough."

The good doctor winced as if Donald had hit him.

"Tell me, Doc. What are the chances that this place can cure me?"

Dr. Havens raised his head slowly. "I can't promise they'll cure you, but they've had some luck in curing stage four cancers." He looked everywhere but at Donald. He opened his jacket and gave him a business card.

Donald yanked the card out of his hand and stuffed into his jacket.

"I'll make a referral," the doctor said softly.

"You do that," Donald growled. He walked out and slammed the door shut.

Traditional medicine wasn't doing a hill worth of beans for him. He had another card that a woman gave him who was supposedly psychic. She'd pleaded with him not to use it unless all other avenues hit dead ends. Well, all other resources had just dried up.

∽

∽

Donald's limo driver pulled up in front of a shady-looking Victorian home in North Denver. This was not the part of town he usually set foot in. Cherry Creek, Aspen, and South Denver were his cup of tea, not anyplace where ten thugs could jump him.

His limo driver, James, got out of the car and opened the door. Donald got out and straightened his suit and ran his hand over his hair. He hadn't shed his hair. Yet. He brushed past James as he headed up the stairs. The only sign on the door that indicated it was a business said come in, but the font reminded him of something out of the Addams Family. He opened the door expecting to find Lurch, but instead walked into New Orleans.

Bright red, purple, and pink walls surrounded him. Beads dangled across the doorway to another room. Voodoo dolls were lined up neatly on one shelf. Below it were bottles of herbs. A third shelf had spell books. Only one of the shelves had any paraphernalia on it. The psychic hadn't mentioned this was a store.

"Good afternoon, Donald," a velvety voice greeted him.

He jerked his head. A young woman had a brightly yellow, red, and orange dhuku wrapped around her head. Large gold earrings dangled from her ears, but it was her dark eyes that drew him to her. It was if she could read his soul.

A knot formed in his belly. He narrowed his eyes. "How did you know my name?"

She gave him a chilling gaze. "I've been expecting you. My name's Madame Mthunzi." She gestured with her arm toward the hallway. "Shall we?"

He crossed his arms over his chest. "Shall we what?"

"Why, find a cure for your cancer?" She edged closer, forcing him to step back. "That's why you're here, isn't it."

"Linda Beck called you–the psychic."

She shook her head. "No. Someone else will be coming soon.

Do you want my help or not? My time is precious and…expensive."

He raised his eyebrow, looking around the room that was in need of a definite upgrade.

"Don't be a fool, Donald. This isn't where I live. I don't mix business with pleasure. Have you decided?"

Another wheezing attack gripped him. Tears filled his eyes and pain tore at his lungs. "Yes…yes."

She straightened and turned her back. "Follow me."

He didn't have any choice but to follow. He took a handkerchief and wiped the spittle from his lips. This was ridiculous. He shouldn't have this disease. He was Donald Elliott—young, vibrant, powerful–not some old man in a nursing home.

Madame Mthunzi led him into a darkened room with a small table, two chairs, and a candle inside a skull that was glittering. Shades covered the windows. She pointed to one of the wooden chairs. "Sit."

He rolled his eyes, not believing he was forced to come to such gibberish.

She shut the door and the candle flickered, casting shadows on the wall. That's when he noticed there were strange markings, which couldn't be good.

She sat across from him. "As I told you before, I'm not cheap."

He glared. "How much?"

"Fifty-thousand dollars."

He gripped the edge of the table tightly. "You're joking?"

She shrugged. "No, I'm not." She lowered her voice. "I know a way to cure you, but it's dangerous."

He lowered his hands. "For who?"

"For both of us." She tilted her head. "That's why there are wards on the wall—to blind their magic."

"Whose magic?"

She smiled sweetly. "Not until I get my money."

"I'll get it to you later—if this works."

"Sorry, it doesn't work that way." She pulled a cell phone out of from underneath the table, which had a magstripe reader to swipe credit cards. "Pay now, or forget it and die."

He met her haughty gaze, and his gut tensed. Fifty thousand wasn't a problem, but he didn't like being bamboozled, either. "How do I know you're not lying to me?"

"You don't."

Pain ripped through his chest and sweat glistened down his temples. Crap, he didn't have a choice. He slowly took out his debit card then slid it through the slot. "This better work."

She took the phone and slid her finger across it. "I'm giving you the information. It will be up to you to make the information work."

"What?" he growled and slowly stood, ready to rip the phone out of her hand. "I just paid fifty thousand dollars for double-talk."

She tilted her chin high. "No. You paid for a cure. I'm giving it to you." She snapped her fingers and pointed toward his chair. "Now, sit."

He slumped back in his chair. She was despicable for preying on his desperation.

"Good." She closed her eyes and moved her palm over the skull. "Spirits of the dead, open the veil, and show us what you know. I command you."

The candle burned brighter, then what looked like a curtain opened on the opposite wall, and a movie started to play.

"Hey, what is this?" Donald clasped the arm of the chair tightly and scanned the room for a movie projector.

"Watch and learn," Madame Mthunzi said.

Donald glared at her, but then looked at the screen. A desert town unfolded. The sun set behind the rugged mountains, turning the clouds purple, pink, and orange. The beautiful sunset, and adobe homes and buildings, reminded him of Sante Fe.

"This is the town of Magic."

"Never heard of it."

"No, you wouldn't. They keep themselves hidden."

The view centered on an adobe home on a ridge. Bushy bougainvillea climbed up one wall of the house and formed an umbrella of shade over the porch. A beautiful dark-haired woman sat on a swing, watching the sunset. She had a tattoo around her neck that reminded him of a dragon. "Who is she?"

"Her name is Gwendolyn Bravian, and she's now married to the Sheriff of New Mexico."

"What's his name?"

"Theo. He doesn't actually have a last name, but he took one for his wife, Gwen."

"So, why am I being shown this?" He clenched his fist. "Like I give a shit."

"Because she's your target."

He stiffened. "Excuse me?"

"She's pregnant."

He leaned back in his chair and scowled. "So?"

"With a dragon."

He blinked, not sure he heard her right. "With what?"

"A dragon."

He sat up straighter. "Are you high?"

She pointed at the wall. "No. See."

Sure enough, a huge yellow and orange dragon landed in front of the house, then transformed into a man wearing a white cowboy hat and a sheriff's uniform. Gwen ran over and wrapped her arms around the man's neck, then kissed him. "This has to be some kind of cheesy Hollywood movie."

"I assure you, Donald, it's not. She's carrying the cure for your illness."

"Explain."

"Dragons carry a great deal of magic. One of their properties is healing. They're the most potent when in utero. If you drink her blood—all of it—you'll be healed."

He wrinkled his nose. "All of her blood?"

"Yes, your cancer is advanced. Within a month, you'll be dead. Only the dragon's blood can heal you. However, only drink it when there's a full moon. This is when the baby's power is the most potent."

"How do I know this isn't bullshit?"

"I've given you what you asked, but there's one more thing. I also need to make you a potion so you can enter Magic. The good witches have put a shield over their little town to keep evil out." Her brown eyes turned completely black. "But I have found a way to penetrate their border. I will also provide you with a book of spells to ward off vampires and witches. You'll also need silver bullets."

"Excuse me?"

"There are shape-shifters and werewolves. Don't you know the lore?"

He scooted the chair back and screeched across the floor. "Why are you doing this?"

"I tried to get into Magic and they turned me away. Now, I'll show them what happens when they cross Madame Mthunzi." She reached into her pocket and pulled on a black stone. "Here take this."

"What is this? More magic?" The stone shimmered in the light as if stars were painted on it.

She shook her head. "No. This stone will help you control the dragon protecting his mate."

"What do you mean?"

"You didn't think you could just waltz in there and kill the pregnant woman, did you?"

Heat flushed over Donald's cheeks. "No, of course not."

"This stone will make him weak."

"You mean it will act the same way kryptonite does to Superman."

She smiled. "Precisely."

"Is the dragon indigenous to Earth?"

"No."

He stuffed the stone in his pocket. "So this really is the dragon's kryptonite."

"Don't be overconfident. He's a dragon, and he'll do everything he can to get the stone away from you. Don't underestimate him."

He patted his pocket. "I won't. Don't worry. Soon there will be one less dragon in Magic. I'm used to getting my way and killing magical creatures to survive won't be a problem."

CHAPTER 2

The same dream came back to Theo…

He was back on Zalara. Now, at least he knew the name of the planet he was from. Like before, dragons flew overhead, chasing each other as if playing a game of tag. Queen Cosmia's three-turret castle loomed in front of him with the same aqua mist hiding its magnificence.

Damon, Queen Cosmia's guard, waited for him at the entrance of the castle. He wore the same leather baldrics that sheathed his sword and space gun. He greeted him at the castle. Instead of his usual sourness, he had a grin. "Welcome back, Theo. Queen Cosima is pleased with you."

"That's comforting. Why have I been summoned?"

His grin faded. "I'm afraid the Queen has had a vision."

Chills whisked down the back of Theo's neck. "By your face, I take it the vision isn't how I can win a million dollars."

"This is no joking manner, Theo." *Once again, Damon went back to the stoic guard.* "Follow me."

Theo reluctantly trailed behind him. Damon's shoulders were stiff and his long blond hair was pulled back in a ponytail. He was a powerful man and loyal to the queen. In the castle's Great Hall, he admired the stars, planets, and galaxies moving around on the ceiling.

Queen Cosima sat on her throne, fingering her silver medallion. Her blonde hair complimented her green eyes. Usually she had a smile for him, but this time, she had a furrowed brow. She dropped her hand and her red gown shimmered. "Whoa, Theo. I bear bad tidings for you."

Theo bowed slightly. "Your Highness." He tilted his head toward Damon. "I gathered that from Mr. Happy."

Cosima shook his head, but didn't answer him. He took his spot next to the queen.

"Evil is coming to you, Theo. A man will come who can destroy your happiness. He also possesses a black stone that comes from Titus. You must retrieve this stone. If you do not, he can use it to destroy you."

"Damon said I had another task. This is it? To obtain the stone."

"This is only part of the task. Your child has many gifts. Only your child can change the stone from darkness to light. You must teach your child how to use these gifts. If you do not, the stone can still shatter not only your happiness, but all of Magic's."

"My baby won't be born for at least eight more months. According to you, the gestation for dragons is longer than humans."

"Quite true," she said.

"Who the hell is this man who is threatens magic?"

"He's already in route. Be prepared, Theo. You'll need help in defeating him. Look to the past."

He frowned. "What the hell does that mean?"

Theo woke with a start, gasping for breath and drenched in sweat. Gwen was snuggled next to him, her bear bottom rubbing against him, and she murmured.

"Theo?" She turned her head. "What's wrong?" She put her hand on his forehead. "Bloody hell, you're sweating. Are you ill?"

"I'm fine." He jerked back. "Stop."

She slowly put her hand down. "I'm sorry. I was just trying to help you."

He sat up, trying to catch his breath, and ran his hand through his hair. "I know. I had a…a dream."

She rubbed his back, her soft caress soothing the angst inside him. "The one about the queen?"

"Yeah." He rubbed the bridge of his nose. He couldn't get her haunting words out of his head.

She scooted closer. "Theo, do you want to talk about it?"

"No, no, I don't." He shook his head.

She glared. "Why not? I'm your mate. I thought you couldna keep anything from me."

He ran his hand down his face. He couldn't tell her, couldn't destroy her happiness, so he lied. His breath came out ragged and his heart was racing. "I just saw dragons burning Magic, and I couldn't take it. There wasn't anything I could do."

"You're strong, Theo. You'd never let anything happen to Magic. I believe in you."

He took her hand and kissed it. Her belief in him never ceased to amaze him. "Thank you. Gwen, in the dream, the Queen told me the name of the planet I'm from."

Her eyes widened. "Really? She did? Which one?" Her voice was as eager as his had been.

"Zalara."

"Zalara? I've never heard of such a planet." Her brows knotted. "Why all of a sudden did she tell you the name of the planet?"

"Because I forgave Hera."

"Anything else?"

He avoided her eyes and tensed. The vein in his cheek quivered. "No." His voice was sharp, but it didn't deter his little mate.

"You're still upset." She wrapped her fingers around his neck. "Let me help you forget, Theo."

"What about the baby?"

"The baby's fine. But I need you."

He took a deep breath, then laid on top of her. His jumping heart bumped hard against his ribs. He stared into her beautiful brown eyes. There was a wildness in them, promising untamed passion, that brought a bead of sweat across his brow. The tattoo on her throat that was the same shape as his, glowed a shimmering orange.

He kissed her parted lips, dominating her, wanting to forget the dream, the warning, the danger…

She slipped her hands around him, her fingers stroking the back of his neck. She wracked her fingers through his hair that always made him mad for her, the tips of her fingernails etching his scalp. Heat spread downward, fanning through his body, erasing the dream. Gwen knew how to distract him, how to ease his worry, how to stir his passion that only she could do.

He moved his hands down her body, stroking and smoothing over her arms, her waist, her hips, knowing what to touch and how to unbridle her passion. Her heart was beating as hard as his. He was hungry for her. He moved his greedily lips over her flesh, licking the salt and ravaging her with a fierce insistence that he knew left her dizzy with need.

"Theo," she cried. Her husky voice was low, laced with enough tension to tendrils of desire down his spine.

"I'll never tire of hearing you call my name," he murmured.

"Take me." She slid her palms down his back.

"Not yet."

He put his lips on her already budded nipple and sucked hard. She arched her back, her nails digging into his shoulders. She parted her thighs, allowing him to press his hips between her.

The dream slipped away until the only thing he could see, feel, and taste was Gwen. He couldn't wait anymore. He lifted his hips and slammed his cock deep inside her hot core. She locked her legs around him. He thrust again and again, and the heat was so fierce, so desperate, the sensations so intense, that he trembled helplessly. She matched his feverish pace, pulling him deeper and deeper inside her. His heart rumbled in his chest, his blood tumbling through his veins, but not so loud he couldn't hear her call out his name. His body consumed all the heat, the power, the ravage fire inside him into swift plunges of his savage hips.

She came in a feverish pitch. With two more hard thrusts, he followed her. He tossed his head back and roared, spilling his seed deep inside her. He collapsed on top of her trembling, laying his head in the curve of her neck.

"Feel better?" She brushed her fingers over his back and kissed his temple.

"You always make me feel better."

But this time, it wasn't exactly true. Queen Cosima said he could lose all those who he loved. He closed his eyes, vowing to protect her and his child. If trouble came to Magic, he'd be ready, even if he had to risk his life to guard his treasure.

CHAPTER 3

*G*wen looked into her husband's beautiful golden eyes and slowly unwound her arms from his thick neck. "How was your day?"

"Uneventful except for the twins playing tricks on Topper. They put Larry underneath one of her hats so when she put it on, she got a big surprise."

She laughed. "Now that's not very smart. Topper's liable to turn both of those boys into flies, so Larry could eat them."

"No, she'd never do that. She loves those two rascals." He put his hand on her belly as his tone turned serious. "How are you doing?"

"Fine. The baby's been active today." She linked her arm through his. "I just donna know if this is normal."

His eyes flashed with concern. "You don't think what we did last night…"

She put her finger on his mouth. "No, silly. We can still have sex for a while. I just don't know if the baby should be this active."

"Why? Based on my research, mothers can feel their babies move the first thirteen and sixteen weeks. It's called a flutter."

Ever since Theo found out she was pregnant, he'd been obsessed with reading baby books, but those were human babies. This was half dragon and half human. "I'm only thirteen weeks along. Besides, I donna know what's normal for a dragon baby."

He clutched her shoulders, his thumbs caressing her. "I know. I don't either. We'll do this together. I promise I'll not let anything happen to you or our child. You're my whole world."

She hugged him, needing to listen to his thumping heart. "And you're mine." She sighed heavily and tears welled in the back of her eyes.

He rubbed her back. "You're thinking of your brother and sister again, aren't you?"

She swallowed to keep from bawling. Another thing with this pregnancy, every two minutes she wanted to burst into tears. Pregnant women were emotional, but this seemed over the top. "I canna help it. I miss them so much."

He kissed the top of her head. "I know. Speaking of Topper, she's coming over tonight."

She lifted her head. "She is? Why?"

He flashed her a smile that always melted her heart. "She has a surprise for you."

"What is it?"

"If I told you, it wouldn't be a surprise, would it?"

She kissed him briefly on the lips. "Did I ever tell you that you're impossible?"

He held her closer and bent his head, his warm breath brushing over her cheeks. "Did I ever tell you how much I love you?"

She parted her lips, and he immediately speared his tongue in her mouth. Her heart pounded wildly as he possessed her. She clutched his shoulders tightly. Theo was her whole life, and she couldn't bear to be parted from him, but that didn't mean she didn't miss Leif and Grace. After their parents had died, they'd only had each other. She didn't even know if they were alive.

She pressed her body against his muscular one, drawing on his strength. His warmth took away the chill she felt which always made her feel safe in his arms. The baby fluttered inside her stomach and she gasped. "Theo?"

"What?" he asked huskily.

"The baby moved." She took his hand and put it her over her belly.

His eyes widened. "I can feel the movement! Do you think the baby was upset over our kissing?"

She laughed. "No, you eejit. But soon we wonna be able to have sex." She clasped his hand and led him toward the house. "So, I think we should finish what we started."

"Your wish is my command."

In their bedroom, she stripped off her clothes. Theo watched her with a lusty gaze.

"I can never stop admiring how beautiful you are," he said.

She lay down on the bed, enjoying watching him unbuttoning his shirt and slowly taking off his pants. He climbed onto the bed and licked and kissed his way up one leg, his calloused finger tips caressing her. The rough stubble on his jaw abraded her flesh. Her limbs and belly quivered with involuntary spasms, and her first orgasm peaked on the horizon.

When he reached the juncture between her thighs, he blew on her curls. The heat of his breath took hers away. He nestled his stubble jaw between her trembling thighs. Tingles glossed over her as she held her breath for the pleasure only he could give her. When he slipped his tongue inside her, she arched off the bed and dug her nails into his broad shoulders. He licked and kissed, feasting on her until she shook, twisting her head side-to-side. A shudder whooshed up her spine and her pulse raced, sending blood down to her core. Gwen spread out her arms, then gasped and gripped the sheets tightly. Sweet shimmers rippled through her body. The skin across her chest tightened and her nipples budded. An orgasm built up inside her, flooding her body with need and warmth.

"Theo!"

He chuckled. "You're almost there, my sweet."

Her heart drummed in her chest, and she bunched up the sheets in her fists.

He left her core and used his tongue to torture her hot flesh. He clamped his hot mouth on her nipple, sucking and swirling his tongue, driving her mad. Every nerve ending was on fire. She ran her fingers through his hair, pressing him against her breast. She arched her back, allowing him to take more of her inside his hot mouth.

He stroked her curls and entered a finger, moving it in and out at a feverish pace. Her first orgasm swept over her and she cried out.

Theo smiled, then put his hands on either side of her. "Now, you're ready."

He climbed up her molten body, his golden eyes flaring with desire.

She parted her lips and he bent his head kissing her, devouring her every gasp. The kiss was one of possession, of love, of fire. Her dragon indulged her every whimper, every moan. His hands slid down her slick body, stirring her into a frenzy. He parted her thighs and then he plunged his cock deep inside her. She arched her hips off the bed and clung to him. She matched his hard thrusts, slamming skin against skin, taking him deeper and deeper until in one fiery moment, her orgasm burst into fragments.

She wrapped her legs around his hips, holding them there. He came and collapsed on top of her. They both lay there, spent and pleasured. He kissed her cheek.

"Tonight, I'll grant your heart's desire."

She panted. "I thought...you...already did."

He kissed her, silencing her curiosity and taking her into another round of bliss.

∽

Gwen finished setting the picnic table, wondering who the guest was that Topper was bringing for dinner. Potato salad, a vegetable tray with ranch dressing, a bowl of summer fruit, and two bags of potato chips were in a neat line.

She picked up another potato chip and popped it into her mouth. She wiped her greasy fingers on her jeans. God, these things were addicting. Back in the seventeenth century, there were fried potatoes, but not these delectable chips.

"You keep eating those and you're going to eat the whole bag."

Theo flipped one of his famous cheeseburgers that were a mix of chorizo and beef. The smell made her mouth water. It wasn't just his hamburgers that made her mouth water. The juncture between her thighs was still sore from their lovemaking. She couldn't wait to feel his hands and lips on her again tonight.

She slid her palms together. "Quit complaining. There's another whole bag left." She rubbed her belly. "Can I help it if the baby loves them?"

"Uh, huh." Theo glanced at his watch. "They'll be here in a few minutes."

She walked over and put her hands on his muscular bicep. "Not even a hint, who is coming?"

"Nope." He grinned and kissed her on the nose. "You wormed some of the surprise out of me, you little minx, but I won't give you all the details."

She cupped his ass hard, and he jumped.

"Gwen," he warned. "You're playing with fire."

"I know." She laughed and walked toward the kitchen to get

the crock-pot full of baked beans. She unplugged the crock-pot when the doorbell rang.

Adrenaline surged through her like lightning. She raced to the front door like a little kid and whipped open the door. Her mouth dropped open and she gripped the door jam tightly. "Oh, my God."

"Gwendolyn. You shouldn't use the Lord's name in vain."

Gwen's chest tingled. She wiped the wetness off her cheeks and laughed. She missed this banter so much. Her identical twin, Grace, stood next to Topper, who was smiling. She held out her arms and Gwen burst into tears.

"I canna believe you're here." Gwen's voice cracked. "I've missed you so much." She hugged her as tight as she could, afraid this was a spell, and Grace would disappear.

Strong arms slowly circled around her waist and she glanced up at Theo. Tears formed at the back of her eyelids. She bit her lip. "How?"

"Me, of course, my dear." Topper brushed past her. She liked to change the color of her hair, and this time it was bright pink. She had swirled it up into a purple clip, making her hair look like an Easter egg.

Grace looked up at Theo and scowled. "Who is this gentleman? And why is he being so forward with you, Gwen? 'Tis not proper."

Gwen clasped Theo's hand and kissed it. "Grace, this is my husband, Theo. Theo, this is my sister, Grace."

Grace curtsied, still wearing a long yellow gown from the seventeenth century complete with a bustle and bonnet. "'Tis a pleasure to meet you, sir." She frowned and covered her mouth. "Gwen, why pray tell, are you wearing such a garment? 'Tis not lady like."

Gwen slid her arm into her sister's and motioned toward her legs. "These are called jeans, Grace. And in this century, they're proper."

Grace frowned. "What's painted on your neck?"

Gwen put her hand on her tattoo. "It's a tattoo, Grace." She looked up at her handsome husband, who always took her breath away. She elbowed Theo in the ribs. "It means I'm mated to this, eejit."

Grace looked at Theo warily. "Mated?"

Gwen laughed and grabbed her sister's hand. "Come into our home. I'm so glad you're here." She stopped. "Is Leif here, too?"

Topper sighed. "No, he was not at Morgana Fey's home. He was away at sea."

Gwen glanced at Theo. "He's with his crew, looking for the demon."

Theo rubbed her back. "He's a dragon and a vampire. He's safe."

Gwen nodded, but heaviness flared in her gut. She remembered his red eyes and the gigantic spider that flung her through time. She shuddered. The demon Zuto was more powerful than anything she'd seen in Magic. She hoped to God Leif was careful.

CHAPTER 4

Theo was parked underneath a shady tree when a red Ferrari convertible whizzed by, flicking dust into the air. He flipped on the screaming siren and chased the red blur that headed toward Magic.

Queen Cosima's warning flashed into his mind. Was this the bastard threatening his wife? He forced himself not to jump to conclusions, but his dragon senses were on high alert.

Heat flushed through his body. His nostrils flared and smoked swirled in the car. The car slowed but didn't immediately pull over. He sped up. The damn fool could run someone over in his sleepy town. Besides, Gwen was taking her sister around to all the residents today and would be in danger. His dragon demanded to be released and he had to take deep breaths to keep it under control. He grabbed his microphone. "Martin, do you read me?"

"Ten four, I read you, Sheriff."

"I'm chasing a red Ferrari–"

"You're kidding? Seriously?"

"Damn it, Martin. Listen, clear Main Street, or this idiot's liable to kill someone."

"Roger and out, Sheriff."

Theo picked up speed, the cruiser shaking and whining. Suddenly, the Ferrari skidded to the side, splattering dust onto Theo's windshield. He slammed on the brakes and jumped out of the car, his gun drawn.

"Roll down the window and put your hands on the wheel now!"

The window rolled down and a young man, who looked like all the meat had been sucked out of him, clutched the steering wheel. "Is there a problem officer?" His innocent voice sent Theo's dragon into a snarling fit.

Suddenly, a blast hit Theo like a slap in the face. He broke out in a hot sweat and he gasped for breath. His hands shook as he held the gun. He The blood drained from his face. He'd never felt anything like it. His strength was slowly being zapped out of him. He spread his shaking legs apart and used his fiercest voice.

"Damn right, there's a problem. Do you know how fast you were going?"

The man shrugged. "No, I was in hurry. Are you feeling okay, Sheriff? You don't look very well."

"I'm fine," Theo growled. He slowly lowered his gun, wondering why the man hadn't been frightened of it. "Where were you going?"

"I think that's my business."

The sun seemed too hot and Theo had trouble concentrating. He drew on his dragon strength, but it seemed to be pint-size rather than dragon-size. "You're in a heap of trouble, Mister. I wouldn't use that arrogant tone with me. Now, driver's license, insurance, and registration."

The man reached over and opened up the glove compartment. He handed Theo the registration and insurance. He opened up his wallet and handed him in his license. "Do you know who I am?"

"No, and I don't care." Theo read his driver's license—Donald Elliott. He'd heard the name, but wasn't going to give the arrogant bastard the satisfaction. Donald Elliott was the heir of Trumpet Computers, but last he read, the man had cancer and his prognosis wasn't good.

Donald narrowed his eyes. "I'm late for an important meeting." The hallow of his cheeks were sunken, and he had dark circles underneath his eyes.

"You're going to be even later—Donald. Up ahead is Magic, which is my town, and you could have killed someone with how fast you were going. Sit here while I radio this in." He walked away, not giving him a chance to argue. He hated to admit it, but he needed to sit in his car.

Martin pulled up next to Theo. "Everything all right, Sheriff? You don't look so good."

Theo glared. "I'm fine."

Today, Martin was a werewolf. He looked like something out of an old horror movie with his ripped shirt and furry face and fangs. As a shape shifter, he could change into anything he wanted for kicks, but his silver eyes were serious. When it came to being a deputy, he took the job sincerely. "Are sure?"

Theo wiped his sweating brow. "I've got it under control." At least he thought he did, but his vision went into tunnel and he thought he'd pass out. He shook his head.

"That the joker tearing up our streets?"

"Yup."

Martin shook his head. He slowly drove passed the red car and released a chilling howl.

The man jumped and bumped his head on the top of his car.

Theo chuckled. He typed in Donald's registration and his driver's record indicated he had numerous speeding tickets, but all of them had been dismissed. He must have a damn good attorney and gotten off on a technicality. Rich, stuck-up bastards always stuck in Theo's craw. Why was Donald here? There were no fancy hotels or resorts. The back of the hair on his neck stood straight-up. Something wasn't right. He had to be the man that

Queen Cosima was warning him about, but he had no way to prove it.

At least not yet.

Ignoring his shaking hands, he wrote out a speeding ticket and walked back to the car nice and slow.

Donald was drumming his fingers on the steering wheel. "Can I go now?"

"Not until you sign this ticket." Theo handed him the clipboard.

"Fine." Donald scribbled his name on it.

Theo gave him back his information. "Drive slow or next time, you'll end up in my jail."

Donald snorted, but didn't argue. He turned on the ignition, gunned the motor, and pulled onto the road.

As soon as he pulled away, Theo stopped shaking and sweating. Crap, Donald had to be the man Queen Cosima was talking about and he had to have the black stone, which obviously turned him into a shrinking dragon.

Theo hurried back to his car and caught up with Donald who was driving the speed limit. As he followed him, the same sinking feelings came over him, but he was determined to find out why Donald was in Magic. Not many people knew of this town, because the witches had put a spell to keep intruders out. Someone had to have invited him in order for him to get past the spell. Theo needed to find out who.

Donald turned down a dirt road that led to The Sleepy Inn, which was managed by a vampire—Byron St. Claire. Byron was a loner and kept to himself, but he'd always followed the laws of Magic.

A yellow Camaro and a silver diesel truck were parked at the two-story adobe inn. Usually, Byron was lucky if he had one customer—let alone three.

Theo pulled along side Donald who jumped out of his car. He marched around to Theo's side.

The same weariness slammed into Theo. He braced himself against the car door.

Although Donald was at least a foot shorter than Theo, he growled, "Are you following me, Sheriff?"

Theo took off his sunglasses. "Yup."

"You're violating my rights."

"You're not under arrest, Donald."

Donald put his shoulders back. "It's Mr. Elliott."

Byron opened the screen door and came down the steps. He had on black sunglasses and a leather jacket.

"Problem, Theo?"

Theo motioned toward Donald and the other two cars. "Your place seems to be busy."

Bryon shrugged and took off his sunglasses. "It's been dead for weeks until Mr. Elliott made reservations. Reserved the whole inn."

"Really?"

Donald glared. "Is there a crime in that, Sheriff?"

Theo met his belligerent stare. "No. But this is a quiet town. Strangers haven't always been a blessing to us."

"I haven't broken any laws."

"No...not yet." But every gut instinct in Theo told him he would.

Donald turned toward Byron. "Now, are you going to check me in or not?"

Bryon rolled his eyes. "Tourists." He leaned close to Theo. "If there is anything suspicious, I'll contact you." He put his famous sunglasses back on and motioned for Donald to follow.

That wasn't very comforting since Bryon hadn't thought anything was wrong when he accepted the booking. But the Sleepy Inn wasn't exactly a money-maker for him, either. It only got busy when Topper had one of her witch's conventions, which wouldn't happen for another three months.

Donald gave him one last glare before he trailed Bryon into the Sleepy Inn.

As soon as Donald disappeared inside, Theo's strength slowly returned. He took a deep breath, then wiped the sweat off his brow. Donald must have the stone, but the problem was that Theo didn't have enough cause to get a search warrant.

He rubbed his chin and then wrote down the Camaro's and truck's license plates. He needed to find out more about Donald and how the hell he'd gotten a hold of the blasted stone. The stone was from Zalara. What was it doing with that asshole? Tingles flickered over his skin and his lungs tightened. Something bad was going to happen, and there was nothing he could do to stop it.

CHAPTER 5

Gwen sat on the veranda with Grace at her favorite Mexican restaurant–Tortilla Flats. Grace had her gown and bustle in a bag. She had on a long yellow beaded dress with a pair of sandals, which was as wild as Gwen could get her to go. She still thought jeans were way too provocative. The only way she would wear the sleeveless dress was if Gwen put on a similar one.

Grace picked up a tortilla chip and examined it. "What do you call this?"

"'Tis a tortilla chip." Gwen picked one up. "You dip it in salsa, which is made from tomatoes and spices."

Grace followed her example and took a bite. Her eyes immediately filled up with tears, and she choked. Gwen got up from her seat and patted her on the back. "Here, drink some water."

Her sister gulped down the water and waved her hand in front of her face like a fan. "Oh my goodness, that was so hot."

Gwen laughed. "I should have warned you. The green one is mild, the red is hot."

"Gwen! Gwen!"

Jonah and Joseph raced down the street toward them, their

cheeks rosy and their eyes full of excitement. The only way she could tell the twins apart was by their black and white hats. Joseph wore black while Jonah white. Unless they decided to switch them.

She tilted her head. "Oh, oh, here comes trouble."

Joseph reached them first. "Beat you." A long pink forked tongue appeared underneath his black hat.

"Naw, I let you win," Jonah insisted.

Grace grabbed Gwen's hand. "What is that underneath the poor boy's hat?"

Joseph grinned and took off his hat. Grace squealed and both boys burst out laughing.

"This is my pet lizard, Larry. He goes with me everywhere I go."

"I see." Grace had her hand over her heart.

"Are you a pirate like Gwen?" Jonah asked.

"Dummy, she's not dressed like one." He frowned. "Why are you wearing a dress, Gwen? You never wear them."

Grace knotted her eyebrows together and clicked her tongue. She ate another chip without dipping it into the salsa.

Gwen smirked. "'Tis the only way I could convince my sister to dress in this century."

"Gwen isn't dressed like a pirate now either, but she's a pirate." He put his hands on his hips. "I'm going to tell Mom you called me a dummy. She says I'm smart."

Joseph rolled his eyes. "Look, genius, she doesn't even have a sword."

Jonah pointed. "Gwen's not wearing one now!"

"Okay, you two. Stop." Gwen gestured with her hand. "This is my twin sister, Grace."

"Cool." Jonah clapped his hand on his brother's shoulder. "You're twins like us. Exactly alike."

"Except for her sister doesn't have a dragon tattoo." Joseph clasped the iron rod. "But you can get one! All you have to do is marry a dragon. Then, you two will be twins and both be married to dragons!"

Grace smiled. "I'm afraid, boys, that my sister isn't a pirate—especially being in the family way." She gave Gwen one of her infamous you're-not-being-ladylike gazes.

"Aw!" Both boys moaned.

Gwen winked. "Despite what my sister says, I'll always be a pirate."

"Yeah!" They both yelled.

"Wow! Look at that!" Joseph's eyes widened and Larry peeked from underneath his hat.

A red Ferrari slowly passed them with dark windows.

Jonah took a step off the curb and the Ferrari gunned its motor. The engine roared and tires squealed.

Gwen jumped up and grabbed the railing. "Jonah! Get back here!"

Dirt spewed into the air and the Ferrari sped off as if hellhounds were chasing it.

Jonah looked at her with his eyes bulging. "Gwen, he wasn't going to stop."

His usual excited voice was quiet and small.

His brother pushed him. "That's cuz you walked out in the middle of the street, dummy."

"Stop calling me that!"

"No, he should have stopped. This is a small town." She picked up her phone.

Theo answered on the first ring.

"Hey."

"Theo, a red sports car almost hit Jonah."

"What? Where?"

"Grace and I were eating at Tortilla Flats when the boys saw us. The car slowed down, then when Jonah stepped into the street, it sped off."

"Is Jonah all right?"

"Yes, he's fine."

"Tell the boys to stay away from that damn car," he growled.

"I will." She hung up. "Boys…"

"We know, we know." Joseph kicked a stone. "We're not supposed to go near the car."

A tall muscular man with short white hair came out of a hardware store.

"Look." Jonah pointed. "There's Frost. Let's go see if he brought anything back from outer space."

The boys tore down the street like mini-hurricanes toward the broad shoulder man.

"Outer space?" Grace sat back in her chair and put her arms over her chest.

"Frost is from the planet Glacier."

Grace raised a delicate eyebrow.

"Donna look at me that way. He's a Star Ranger and married to a witch. No one in this town is who you think they are. There are witches, vampires, werewolves, trolls, fairies…"

"Except for you," Grace said quietly. "We're just normal folk."

"I know." Gwen bit her lip. "That's what scares me, Grace. I'm pregnant with a dragon. Did I tell you that Theo's from the planet Zalara?"

Gwen put her hand on her chest. "You're married to someone from the heavens?"

"No, Gwen. From outside of Earth. Theo's planet is filled with dragons." She lowered her head. "I donna have any mystical powers. What if I canna carry this baby?" Tears formed behind her eyes and her throat dried up. "What if something happens?"

Grace took her hand and squeezed it gently. "I know you're scared. That's why I'm here. We'll figure this out together."

Gwen forced a smile. "Thank you. I just wish Leif were here."

Grace sighed. "He's off on his pirate ship determined to kill the demon. I was angry with him for leaving his pregnant wife,

Isabella, but I've come to trust the witch Morgana Fey. She's in good hands. My task is here with you."

"Thank you." She glanced up and their waiter was carrying two plates of their steaming food. "Our food's here, and I'm starved."

Their waiter, Juan, placed the tray on the edge of the table. "Chile rellenos?"

Gwen raised her hand. "That's me." The smell of roasted peppers, melted cheese, and hot black beans, made her stomach growl. She picked up her fork and cut a big slice of the Chile relleno that was smothered with guacamole. The baby flipped in her stomach and Gwen didn't know if it was for excitement or dread.

Grace picked up her fork and poked at her food. "What did you call this again?"

"A chicken burrito. You'll like it. Try it."

She shrugged and took a dainty bite of the burrito. Her eyes widened. "Oh my, this is delicious."

Gwen swallowed her bite, the cheese and spicy pepper warming her throat and belly as she waited for the baby's response. The baby was more active. She hoped that was a good sign and cut another slice of the stuffed relleno.

"Can I try yours?" Grace looked at Gwen's plate.

"Sure." She scooted her plate toward Gwen.

Her sister dipped her spoon and scooped up a small bite. "That's spicy. Do you think 'tis good for the baby?"

Gwen put her hand on her belly. "She's very active and my stomach's fine."

"Good." Grace patted her mouth. "I need to use the ladies' powder room. Where is it?"

"The powder rooms are called restrooms." She tilted her head. "'Tis right on the other side of the bar."

"If you'll excuse me." Grace neatly folded her napkin and put it to the side of her plate. "I'll be right back."

Gwen nodded as she took a bite of her black beans. She sipped some water, wishing it were a Margarita. Since she'd been in Magic, she'd grown quite fond of tequila. She sighed. No drinking for a year.

Cars rolled down the street, but there was no sign of the red sports car or Theo. Maybe he'd found the car and given the driver a ticket. She scooped up her black beans with a tortilla chip and then a dabbed it with guacamole–the perfect bite.

After a few minutes, she realized half her plate was gone and Grace hadn't returned. Maybe she'd gotten sick. Mexican food was much spicer than the bland food she'd be used to eating in the seventeenth century. She should have taken her sister somewhere different.

She reluctantly pushed her chair away from the table.

Juan hurried over. "Is everything all right, no?" His eyes were filled with worry.

"Aye, the food is delicious. I just need to check on my sister. Donna take the dishes."

He smiled. "Sì, Señora."

Gwen hurried to the restroom and opened the wooden door. Her sandals clicked across the reddish-brown toccata tile. The granite counter had a box of tissue and a soap dispenser in the shape of a cactus. Soft lights glowed and Gwen could see her worried face in the mirror. She looked so different in the yellow dress. She was much more comfortable in jeans and cowboy boots.

"Grace? Are you ill?" Three stalls were in the small bathroom. She checked for Grace's sandals, but quickly realized Grace wasn't in the bathroom. A chill wavered down her spine. How could she have missed her? The restaurant wasn't that big and not many people were in the bar. Most people were sitting outside on the patio.

She hurried back to their table, but Grace wasn't there. She motioned to Juan. "Did you see where my sister went?"

He shook his dark head. "No, I didn't. I'm sorry."

The hairs on the back of Gwen's neck rose and goose bumps broke out on her arms. Something was wrong. This wasn't like Grace. She'd never leave without telling her.

Gwen hurried to the front of the restaurant. The hostess, a young woman with her hair pulled up into a bun, stood behind a podium that faced the double doors.

"Excuse me?"

The woman smiled. "What can I do for you?"

"Did you see a woman dressed like me leave here?"

The hostess smiled. "Yes. She left with her husband and his friend. Her husband said she wasn't feeling well."

Gwen's legs shook and her heartbeat spiked. "My sister doesna have a husband. Where did they go?"

"They just left a few minutes ago."

Gwen bolted out the double doors. "Grace?" She looked down the street, but didn't see her sister. Across the street, Jonah and Joseph were in the park, chasing each other round the swing sets. She raced over toward them. "Jonah, Joseph, did you see my sister?" Her frantic voice stopped them in their tracks.

Larry peeked from underneath Josoph's hat. Joseph pointed down the road. "You didn't tell us she was married like you."

"Yeah, she went with her husband. She didn't look good. Her face was really pale. What she'd eat in there that made her so sick?"

"Grace isn't married. Did she walk down the street?"

"No." Jonah shook his head. "They got into a huge silver truck and took off."

Joseph's eyes widened. "You mean your sister's been kidnapped?"

"Aye. Go get Topper. I've got to call Theo." She raced back into the restaurant to snatch her phone.

Once again, he answered. "Gwen..."

Gwen ran her shaking hand through her hair. "Theo, Grace

has been kidnapped! Two men forced her out of the bar. I didna see it happen, but Jonah and Joseph saw her leave. They said the men and Grace left in a silver truck."

"Damn it, I knew the man was trouble. The Queen was right." His voice rippled with frustration.

Her belly twisted into a knot. "What do you mean? This has something to do with your dream, doesna it?"

He didn't answer her right away.

"Theo, answer me!"

"I don't know if the man has anything to do with my dream or not, okay?"

"Okay."

"Look, earlier I pulled over this man driving the red Ferrari. When I got near the car, something happened."

Her hand was shaking as she held the phone. "Like what?"

"I got really weak as if something sucked out all my strength. I've never felt anything like that before."

"How could this happen? You're a dragon."

"Tell me about it."

"What was this man's name? Where'd he come from?"

"His name was Donald Elliott, and he's from Denver. He was speeding like a bat out of hell. I followed him to the Sleepy Inn where there was a yellow Camaro and a silver pick-up. I ran the plates on both of them."

Gwen gripped her phone tighter. "Who were they?"

"Rick Mason and Shawn Whitehead. Two ex-cons. They served together in Canon City outside of Denver."

"Why didna you arrest them?" Her voice was so loud people at the restaurant were staring at her, but she didn't care. If she was in the seventeenth century, Leif would have cut down the two convicts—no questions asked.

"On what charges, Gwen? I couldn't do anything until they committed a crime." His scolding tone sent the hairs on the back of her neck standing straight up.

Tears formed on the back of her eyelids. Her stomach quivered and she didn't know if it were her being upset or the baby moving. "Well, they just did. They kidnapped my sister. And 'tis all your fault."

He sighed heavily. She paced back and forth on the street, images of what those men could be doing to her sweet sister. Grace wasn't a fighter. She was a gentle soul.

"Gwen, I'm sorry. Don't move. I'm on my way. Don't go anywhere near Mason or Whitehead."

"Fine." She clicked off her phone, not having any intention of staying put. How could Theo have done this? He was the sheriff and should have been protecting the town from ruffians. This wasn't the first time she'd dealt with men like them who had threatened her sister. She'd been protecting her sister all of her life. Her brother Leif let her down to go off pirating, forcing her to be the protector of the family. And now her darling husband had just put her back in the same situation.

But what scared her all the way down to her toes, was why did Theo get weak around this man? Was there dark magic at work? Could the man kill him? She had to do something. This gang of ruffians weren't going to murder her sister and her husband.

She narrowed her eyes. No problem, she was ready. She was a pirate and would make mincemeat of those bastards if they harmed one hair on her sister's head or made a move against her mate.

CHAPTER 6

*D*onald drummed his fingers on the table and stared at the unconscious woman across from him. Not wanting the good sheriff to find them, he'd rented a three-room cabin up in the hills. He'd preferred the little inn, but not with the nosy sheriff poking around.

Luckily, Madame Mthunzi had given him hex bags. He'd put them in all the corners of the house like she'd instructed and when he did, the house turned invisible. Let the damn sheriff try and find them now.

A potbelly stove flickered in the corner. He'd laid out all the tools he needed on the kitchen counter to kill this poor woman–a narrow five inch bone knife, a butcher knife, a meat cleaver, a twenty-five inch bone saw and a heavy duty meat cleaver. When he was a kid, his dad had taken him hunting and taught him how to butcher a deer. He never thought he would end up butchering a beautiful woman, but he didn't have a choice. She was his last hope to not die a lingering, painful death.

Her dark head was slumped over to the side. His two goons, Rick Mason and Shawn Whitehead, had forced her out of the restaurant at gunpoint, then used chloroform to knock her out.

He rubbed the bridge of his nose. Maybe he was losing his mind. So far, since he'd been in this small backward town, he hadn't seen anything that made him suspect the residents were anything but the local yahoos.

He broke out in a loud cough that squeezed his lungs and made his eyes tear up.

When he stopped, the woman was staring at him, but she didn't have gold eyes.

"I'm surrounded by idiots," he mumbled.

She frowned and pulled on her restraints. "Who are you?"

He slammed his fist down on the table hard. "Mason!"

The woman jumped.

A burly red bearded man hurried over from another room. "Yes, boss?"

Donald narrowed his eyes. "Didn't I say the color of her eyes would be gold?"

Mason scratched his beard, then shrugged. "But in the light, it was hard to tell."

Donald motioned. "Look."

He took a step closer.

"Stay away from me!" The woman leaned back into her chair as if trying to disappear.

He hung his head. "Crap, you're right. They're brown."

"Yes, I know, genius."

The woman struggled in the chair and bit her lip. "What do you want with Gwendolyn?"

"That's none of your concern," Donald said.

She sat stiffly. "I'm afraid it does, sir. She's my sister."

"See, boss?" Mason flicked his hand over his bald head. "They're twins. Anybody could make a mistake."

Donald rolled his eyes. "You mean any moron. Now, you're going to correct this, aren't you?"

"You want to exchange her for the other one?"

He smiled, revealing all of his teeth. "No, but we're going to have *her* come to us."

The woman glared. "Please, sir, leave her alone! She's in the family way."

He walked over to her. Her eyes grew larger, and she pulled on her restraints.

"Get away from me."

"What is your name?" He put his hand on the back of her head, then stroked her hair.

"I must insist that you release me this minute."

He wrapped his fingers in her thick hair and yanked hard. "I asked you a question."

She gasped, her lower lip trembled. "Grace."

He loosened his grip. "Now, Grace, this is what you're going to do. I'm going to call your sister and you're going to say exactly what I want you to say."

"And if I donna?"

He snapped his fingers.

Mason ripped out a knife from his belt and immediately put it under Grace's throat, forcing her to tilt her head back.

Donald whispered into her ear. "Then, my associate will slice your pretty little neck. Do you understand me?"

"Aye." Her voice was so low he could barely hear her.

He tilted his head at Mason who slowly lowered his knife. He released her hair and waited for her to go into hysterics and plead for hers and her sister's life, but she disappointed him. She gave him an intense, fevered stare. Her face was tight and her skin stretched into a snarl. If she were a cat, she would have leaped at him and scratched his eyes out with her claws.

His scalp prickled, and for one moment, he regretted kidnapping her. His lungs tightened and he gasped to breathe. He broke into another fit of coughing, and he gripped the back of her chair to steady himself. Tears blurred his vision and his body shook.

The attack lessened and he could breathe slowly, but his chest hurt as if someone had turned a tourniquet on his lungs. He was running out of time–back to the plan.

In a low voice, he asked, "Now, what's your sister's phone number?"

"I donna know, Sir."

His pulse elevated. "Wrong answer." He slapped her hard across the face.

Her head swung to the side, her hair flying all around.

"Now, I am going to ask you again. What's your sister's number?"

She raised her head, her hair shielding her face. "I donna know."

He gritted his teeth. "Bitch!" He back-handed her again.

She cried out. Her head swung to the other side.

"I donna know."

He grabbed her hair and yanked. "I could do this all day. I'm going to ask you one more time. What is your sister's phone number?"

"I...I donna know. I donna know what a phone number is. Please...please stop."

He twisted his fingers tighter. "What the hell do you mean?"

"I came...I came from the seventeenth century."

He released her. "Liar!" He scraped his hand over his face. "If you don't tell me what I want to know, I'll let Mason and Whitehead have their way with you."

"No, please!" Her voice shook and she lost her defiance. "Topper–a witch–came and brought me back through time. I swear 'tis true."

"Then, tell me what I want to know." He grabbed her trembling shoulders and dug his fingers into her flesh.

"I donna know." She hung her head and sobbed.

He dropped his hands. "You're not giving me much of a choice."

Mason licked his lips and flashed his gaze over Grace.

Donald's stomach tightened. Usually he wouldn't have anything to do with scum like Mason and Whitehead, but he was a desperate man and desperation made him do things he'd never do.

He wanted to live.

Mason ripped the top of Grace's dress. She screamed and threw her head back.

Donald blinked his eyes. She wore an old fashioned corset. He'd seen corsets before, but this was one was faded and the material was different. Really old fashioned like seventeenth century old fashioned. Mason slipped his hand down her corset and she spat on his face. He punched her, snapping her head back. "You be nice. Or you'll not like what we'll do to you."

Tears streaked down her cheeks. Her lip was cut and swelled up. Blood trickled down the corner of her mouth.

Maybe she was telling the truth and was from the seventeenth century. He hadn't believed dragons existed until he met Madame Mthunzi. Donald held up his hand. "Wait."

Mason groaned but withdrew his hand from inside the corset. His fingernails were longer than a man should have and Donald bet Grace had scratches down her breast, but she had brought this on herself. She should have been more cooperative.

He wedged himself in between Mason and Grace. He knelt and put his hands on her trembling knees. "Do you know where she lives?"

She looked warily at Mason, then sniffed. "I donna know the address, but they live on top of a plateau that looks down on Magic. Gwen said 'tis the only house with pink bougainvillea in full bloom that grows over their door way."

Donald stood. He glared at Mason. "Now, can you two idiots find this house on the plateau?"

Whitehead shrugged his shoulders. "What's a bougnaveila?"

"It's pronounced bougainvillea, you moron. It's a flower."

Donald took out his phone and found a picture of the pink flowered plant. "This is what it looks like."

Whitehead looked at the screen. "Oh. I know them flowers. Just never knew what theys was called."

Donald flicked his hand. "Now go. Both of you. Don't come back until you have the bitch. And this time, she'd better have a dragon tattoo."

Mason ogled Grace, but reluctantly followed Whitehead out the door.

Donald sat in a chair across from Grace. "You better not be lying. Next time, I won't stop them. Do you understand me?"

She nodded silently. Her dark hair hung in her face. Unlike the other women in town, she didn't have any make-up on, since her tears hadn't smeared her mascara and eye-shadow. She could have been wearing waterproof make-up, but he didn't think so. Her lips were cracked as if they hadn't been moisturized. Still, she was beautiful. Too bad he had to kill her. Donald couldn't afford any loose ends.

CHAPTER 7

*G*wen changed into her shirt, jeans, and boots, her hands shaking. Her muscles and veins strained against her skin. Damn, Theo! Why did he have to follow the rules? Magic was supposed to be a safe place. 'Twas his job to make sure everyone was safe–including her sister.

If anything happened to Grace, she'd never forgive them. He should have had both of those two men followed, especially if he smelled trouble.

Her stomach flipped-flopped angrily and she rushed to the bathroom, emptying lunch. She wiped off her mouth with a towel. She took a swig of water and swooshed it around in her mouth. She spat it out into the sink.

"Now, little...one," she panted. "We've got a job to do. Your aunt's in trouble. We have to save her. So, work with me on this, will you?"

She put her hand over her fluttering stomach and prayed she wouldn't get sick again. She waited another moment before she headed into the living room.

She yanked the sword off the fireplace, then went to the gun cabinet to get her sheath and Colt single action revolvers. Theo's weapons were superior to hers, but she wasn't comfortable with them. The Colts felt more like her flintlocks, but obviously with better accuracy. She quickly loaded each of them and slid them into her holster.

She caught her reflection in their dresser mirror, but instead of looking like a seventeenth century pirate, she looked like a biker pirate with her leather jacket. She wished she had powers like Topper so she could really kick some ass, but she was only human.

She'd learned to fight on the mean streets of London back in the seventeenth century, so she wasn't a pansy-ass, either. "Donna worry, Grace. I'm coming."

If they made her sister cry, she'd blow a hole right in the middle of their forehead.

She opened the door to two burly bearded men standing on her porch. Behind them was a silver truck. Her stomach fluttered as if a million butterflies were ramming to get out.

The tall red-bearded man cast his gaze over her. "See, Whitehead, this one's got a tattoo on her neck."

Gwen froze. They were the two convicts–Rick Manson and Shawn Whitehead–Theo had told her about, and they were standing on her porch. She slowly moved her hand over her Colt. "Who are you?"

"You need to come with us." Whitehead–the shorter blond man–reached for her.

But she was faster. Gwen knocked his hand away from her. His eyes widened in surprise. She unleashed her sword and pulled out her revolver.

They reached for their guns, but she shook her head. "I wouldna if I were you. I really wouldna. Before you even fired a shot, you'd both be dead."

They glared, but did as she asked. The convicts were twice as tall as she was and could easily overpower her if given half a chance. She wished Theo would drive up, but she was on her own.

"Now, I'm going to ask again." She pushed the tip of the sword underneath Manson's chin. "I'm not going to ask a third time."

His green eyes bulged.

Whitehead stared at her Colt. "She ain't like the other one."

Gwen smirked. "No, I'm not. What did you two bastards do with my sister?"

Whitehead glared. "If ya dudden come with us, he's fixin' to kill her."

She narrowed her eyes. "Who?"

The two men glanced at each other.

She pressed the tip of the sword deeper into Mason's hairy neck. "I said who?"

"Elliott. Donald Elliott," he gasped, spit rolling down the sides of his mouth and staining his beard.

"What does he want with my sister?"

Whitehead shook his head. "He dudden want her. He wants you."

She frowned. "Why?"

He shrugged. "We dudden know."

His eyes shifted and he looked down at his boots. He was lying.

She pulled the trigger. "Where is he?"

"He dun buried in a cabin tighter than a Colorado tick," Whitehead blurted.

"There are lots of cabins around here. What's the name of the road?"

"I dudden know the name of the damn road, but it ain't far from here," he said. "Elliott said that if you dudden come, he's fixin' to kill your sister."

"Well, I wouldna want to disappoint him."

"That's what we were going to do, bitch," Mason snarled.

"Donna make me mad." She forced his head back even further, a trickle of blood rolled down his neck.

He put his hands up. "All right, all right. Just don't cut my damn throat."

"Move," she said. "Hands in the air."

Both men grumbled, but obeyed. She followed them out to the truck when she discovered a real problem. There was no way she could climb into the crew cab truck while holding onto her weapons. She had to come up with a plan.

She tilted her head. "Open the back door."

Whitehead glanced at Mason who smiled. "Use it."

She slowly pulled back the trigger. "Use what?"

"Kryptonite."

"I think you've watched too many Superman movies."

Whitehead laughed and reached into his pocket. He pulled out a shimmering stone that had sparkling stars.

She cried out. An invisible forced slammed into her, and she staggered as if someone punched her in the gut. Sharp pain twisted in her stomach and she fell on her knees. The sky, cactus, and mountains stirred around her. "Bloody hell."

Whitehead sneered. "You still think that bitch?" He tossed the stone up in the air and caught it.

Mason scratched his temple. "Well, I'll be damned. It does work."

The agony shot up, but a weariness gripped her as if all of her limbs had turned to cannon. "What's…what's happening to me?"

"Get the bitch in the car," Mason growled. He swung open the passenger door.

"Leave me alone!" She protectively put her shaking arms around her queasy stomach.

Whitehead grabbed her arm and yanked her off the floor. He tossed her into the car like she was a sack of potatoes. In the next minute, he was on top of her pinning her arms behind her and tying up her wrists.

"You move and you won't like what happens," he warned.

His hot breath hissed on her neck and she shivered.

Her heart beat wildly, but she turned her head and met his deadly stare. "No, you wonna like what will happen." 'Twas a lie, but they didn't know that.

Whitehead lost his sneer and climbed off her. She rolled onto her back and slammed her foot into his chin. He smacked against the other window.

He rubbed his chin. Hate flared in his eyes. "You're gonna pay for that bitch!" He balled up his fist and smashed it into her face. Pain sizzled through her. White stars floated around her eyes.

Whitehead yanked her shirt. "Now, listen good. I ain't gonna take nothing from some dumb whore."

"Go to hell." She spat in his face.

She should have stopped, but being a mild hostage wasn't in her cards.

He hit her again hard. The stars stopped spinning and his face disappeared, then only darkness.

CHAPTER 8

Theo skidded the squad car in front of Tortilla Flats. He got out of the car and slammed the door hard. "Gwen!"

Pain swelled in the back of the throat at Gwen being so mad at him. He should have put a tail on Mason and Whitehead, but both he and Martin had been busy at a multiple car accident on the edge of town. He and Theo were it on Magic's police force.

People, sitting on the patio, stopped eating and stared at him uneasily. Jonah and Joseph came barreling out of the restaurant.

Martin pulled up behind him. "Sheriff, wait."

The twins raced toward him, waving their arms. "Theo! Theo!"

Heat flushed through his body. He held up his hand. "I don't have time for this." He swerved around Jonah.

"Gwen's not here." Jonah grabbed his arm.

Joseph stepped in front of him. "Neither's her sister."

Theo growled. "How do you know?" He grabbed Joseph by the shirt and Larry peeked from underneath Joseph's hat.

Joseph put his hand on Theo's. "We don't know. Please don't hurt me." His voice was so small and his eyes so huge that calmness penetrated Theo's anger.

"Are you really going to hurt those sweet boys?" A familiar female voice asked.

Theo whirled around. Topper held a book in her hand and a wand in another. Her hair was bright blue and pulled back into a neat ponytail.

"What's going on Topper?"

She frowned and looked at her book. "Bad magic, I'm afraid."

Theo scowled. "What do you mean? Where the hell is she?"

"Unfortunately, Theo, I can't track her. Bad Voodoo is at work here."

"Fine. I know where to start."

"Theo, wait," she said. "I sense something else besides magic. I've never felt anything like it before."

"Damn it, Topper. What is it?"

She folded her arms across her chest. "Yelling at me isn't helping."

"I'm sorry, but Gwen…She's my life."

"I know, Theo, but you're going to need help. I fear if you don't, something awful will happen."

"I can find my woman." Theo got into the car and turned on the siren. He sped over to the Sleepy Inn.

Byron walked out of the main office, wearing his famous sunglasses and leather jacket. "Hi Theo. What can I do for you?"

"Where are your guests?"

Byron shrugged. "They left. Still paid for the week though."

Theo pressed his arms to his side to keep from tearing Byron apart. "I thought you were going to contact me if anything strange happened."

Byron took a step backward. "I didn't think guests checking out of here was strange."

"Did they say where they were going?"

"No." He shook his head.

Theo slammed his hand on the top of his roof, making a dent. "Damn it."

Byron jumped and his face turned ashen. "Calm down, Theo."

Theo put his hands up in the air. Smoke puffed out of his flaring nostrils. "Did you at least see which direction they went?"

"No. I'm sorry."

Theo hopped back into his car and peeled out of the parking lot, spraying gravel and dirt. Byron held up his arm to shield his face. He ran back into the hotel as if he were afraid he'd burst into flames.

Sweat rolled down Theo's temples. He gripped the steering wheel tight. God knows what Gwen would do. His little pirate wench had a definite mind of her own. He had to find her before she did something really stupid or worse get herself killed. Her love for her sister ran deep and she'd do anything to save her.

A flutter lit up in his gut. Maybe she was home. He raced home, weaving out of traffic. He thought about changing into a dragon, but his blood was burning and pounding between his ears. He could barely control his anger. There was no way on Earth he could control his dragon's fury. If he transformed, he'd liable burn the town to the ground hunting for his stubborn wench.

He called her cell phone one more time.

"Hello, this is Gwen..."

He immediately hung up and tossed his phone onto the passenger seat. It wasn't like her not to answer the phone–especially when he called.

The hair on the back of his neck raised up. She was in trouble. He knew it.

He skidded the car into the driveway. He bolted out of the car and into the house. "Gwen, Gwen? Are you here?"

The kitchen and dining room were empty, but what made his heart sick, was the seventeenth century cross-hilted sword over the fireplace mantel was missing.

"Jeezuz, Gwen."

He hurried over to the gun safe and opened it. He bowed his

head. Her Colts were both missing. He shut the door and spun the dial. "What fool thing have you done, woman?"

He had to find her. He just had to. She was in trouble. Every bone in his body tensed with dread.

He grabbed one of her shirts and inhaled her sweetness.

Concentrate, damn it.

He wasn't good at finding her by scent unless he was calm. Heat swelled inside him and his skin tingled. He lowered the shirt and sucked in deep breaths. His vision clouded and his muscles rippled, the dragon fighting to come out.

He shook his head. "No." Without Gwen, he always struggled to control his dragon. Her sweet kiss and touch calmed the beast inside him.

Now, concentrate.

Nothing.

Maybe he needed to be outside. Their front porch looked over Magic and just maybe he could catch her scent.

He came to an abrupt stop. He wasn't alone.

"I told you, you're going to need help." Topper stood next to three other men. Two of them he knew. One was his deputy and the other was Cè Jackman, a vampire pirate. Cè had been flung through the time by a giant spider in the seventeenth century like Theo's wife, but now he was the local furniture maker.

He had a holster with his guns and his sword. His blond hair was pulled back and he'd a sheepish grin. "You really want to do this on your own?"

"Maybe." He sized up the other large man that he had no clue who he was. He had a long dark hair and green eyes and wide shoulders, and he was dressed like a pirate.

Topper turned to the third man. "This is Leif Black."

Theo frowned. "You're Gwen's and Grace's brother?"

"Aye. I am. The witch came and got me when I was out of sea." He smirked. "She didna give me much choice."

Topper put her hands on her hips. "Your sisters are in danger."

"I know. They're my life. There's nothing I willna do for them."

Theo bared his teeth. "And so how are these men going to help me?"

"Didn't Gwen tell you?" Topper stuck her thumb out of Leif. "Her brother is a dragon, and he knows how to control his beast."

Theo stiffened. "I'm in control."

Topper raised her eyebrow. "Really? Have you picked up Gwen's scent?"

Theo's neck and ears turned hot. "I was coming out here to see if I could a get a good whiff."

"I can find my woman anywhere," Leif said. "But you have to be calm."

"I am calm!" Theo growled and gnashed his teeth.

"Uh, uh." Topper gave him a knowing stare. "I can see that."

Martin looked down at his hairy feet. Cè held his stare without flinching.

"I know you're worried," Topper said. "We all are. But luckily, I brought something that might help." She pulled a green bottle out of her leather purse. "This is a calming elixir."

"Only Gwen can calm me," he muttered.

"Yes, I know, Sheriff." She walked over to him. "This contains her essence." She handed it to him. "Now, drink."

He reluctantly took the vile from her and unscrewed the black top. He sniffed. An immediate smell of exotic flowers filled his nostrils. The knotted muscles balled up in his neck and shoulders slowly unwound. Topper gave him a superior smile and he grimaced.

But she was right. He did need help. This was no time to hold on to stiff-necked pride–not with Gwen's life hanging in the balance.

He downed the elixir in one gulp. Surprisingly, it tasted sweet and spicy at the same time, like his Gwen. The tightness in his chest lessened, and he could breathe.

Topper rubbed his arm. "Feel better."

"Actually, I do."

She flashed him a fixed stare. "You sound skeptical? You know my spells never fail."

"Close your eyes," Leif said. "Then sniff. Trust me, it works."

He did as his brother in-law asked. He inhaled deeply, blocking out everything in his mind. The aroma of the bougainvillea teased him. Gwen had planted those. The desert breeze whiffed over him of cacti, cooking smells–someone was barbecuing ribs–a bubbling brook and then a powerful smell slammed into him of sweetness, spice, and fear. He flew open his eyes.

His nostrils flared and smoke puffed out. "She's nearby. And she's scared. We have to go now."

Topper grabbed his arm. "No."

He jerked free. "Why?"

Topper gestured toward the other men. "You're not at full strength. Not yet. You need to wait for the full moon."

He scrubbed a hand over his face. "She could be dead by then."

"Theo, I've told you there's dark magic at work. If you rush in now, the magic could kill you and Gwen. Is that what you want?" Her voice softened.

"No, of course not. Then what do we do?"

"You form a plan," she said. "Unfortunately, I can't help you. The dark magic will smite down any witch from Magic. Whatever spell I try to use, it will magnify on me. But with the combined forces of two dragons, a vampire, and a shape-shifter, you can overcome the evil. You must work together. When the moon is full, you'll be at full strength."

"Will Gwen still be alive?"

"Yes," Topper said. "He must wait to kill her during the full moon, because that's when your baby's gift is at full strength. You must tell Gwen to unleash her baby's abilities."

"What do you mean?"

"I have just discovered that space dragon babies are very powerful, especially in the womb, but they don't know it until they're are called upon."

Theo's gut tightened. "That's why he wants to kill her, isn't it?"

"I'm afraid so. I have one more piece of advice. In this battle, you must trust all of your senses and not just your sight. Your sight may betray you. You all possess superior senses, especially smell. You'll find this one will be your most powerful."

Martin frowned. "What does that mean? We're supposed to go around Magic sniffing like bloodhounds?"

Topper pinched his cheek. "Maybe you should, shape-shifter. I have a feeling where they're holding Gwen isn't too far from here. I must leave and consult with the council. We need to figure out way to get this dark presence out of Magic before it spreads like a cancer."

"Have you discovered something?"

"Not yet. But for what I can detect, I'm not sure it's magic. It's strong." She headed toward her car and left them all staring at each other.

Theo rubbed his chin. "Before we can form a plan, we need to find their hideout. A bloodhound wouldn't be a bad idea."

Martin rolled his eyes. "God, the things I'll do for you, Sheriff. You know, I prefer a werewolf…"

Theo lifted his chin and growled.

Martin put his hands up. "All right, all right. Don't fry my ass. …Give me something of Gwen's, so I can catch her scent."

Theo motioned. "Follow me."

Martin, Cè, and Leif followed him back into the house. Theo

picked up one of Gwen's favorite blankets and handed it to Martin.

Martin held it up to his nose and smelled. He tossed it back onto the couch. "I've got it." The long hair on his face and body decreased and turned from brown to red. His short-haired fur coat hung loose around his head and neck. The skin fell into loose, pendulous ridges and folds. His height shrunk until he was a little over two feet tall. His shirt and pants disappeared. He panted, slobber dripping from his jowls.

Theo smiled. "Best damn looking bloodhound, I've ever seen." He bent down to pet him.

Martin growled and bared his teeth.

"Easy, deputy. This is what I want you to do. Go find Gwen, then report back here. Topper said she was close by."

Leif opened the door. "Find them. I need my sisters to be safe." He closed it. "Now, what?"

Theo looked at both Leif and Cé. "We form a plan."

CHAPTER 9

*G*wen woke to a splitting headache. She couldn't see out of her right eye. Mason had hit her hard. She'd no idea those two lumbering eejits could move that fast.

"Mason shouldn't have hit you," a wheezy voice said.

A man sat in a recliner facing a roaring fireplace, which was strange since it was hotter than hell outside. Even at dusk, the temperature in Magic was still hot. She didn't see Grace or the two convicts, either.

"Are you Elliott?"

"Yes, I am." He broke out into dry cough that almost made her feel sorry for him.

Almost.

"Let me go, you cur." Gwen pulled on her restraints and twisted in her chair. A log fell off in the fireplace and sparks flew.

Donald sat at a chair and patted his mouth. "This will all be over soon."

"Where is my sister?"

Donald hacked and hacked then spit up into his handkerchief. He jerked his thumb toward another room. "She's...unconscious."

"You have me. Why havena you let my sister go?"

He swiveled his leather recliner to face her. "Because I can't have any witnesses."

His face was racked with pain and his eyes were sunken in his skull. He looked like a starving skeleton except for his full head of hair.

She pulled on her restraints. "Why are you doing this?"

"I'm dying. And you're my last resort."

Beads of sweat formed on the top of her forehead. "What do you mean?"

"A Voodoo priestess said that the blood of a dragon could cure me."

"You bloody codfish. I'm not a dragon."

"I know, but you're pregnant with one. The priestess said dragons are the most powerful when they are in utero. I wished this hadn't become so drastic, but I didn't have a choice."

She gripped the arms of her chair tightly. "What do you mean?"

"Your baby is most powerful when it's midnight." He walked over to the small kitchen and ran his hand over a white towel that had tools underneath it. He ripped back the towel to reveal a long and a short knife, an ax, a saw, and a heavy-duty meat cleaver. That's when I have to kill you and drain all your blood."

Her mouth ran dry and the room, tools, and his face spun around her. Heat spiked inside her and she fought not to pass out. "You're the spawn o' the devil."

"No, I'm a dedicated businessman. I don't deserve this disease. I deserve to live."

She frowned. "And my baby and I deserve to die?"

"Your baby isn't human, so I'm only putting down an animal. However, regrettably, I have to put down both you and your sister."

"No." She struggled harder. "You canna be serious. Drinking my blood isn't going to heal you."

Evil flickered in his eyes and he licked his lips. "Not yours. Your baby's."

Her stomach fluttered as if the baby heard what he was saying. Maybe he or she could hear. 'Tis not like she had a baby dragon reference book. "You'll never touch my baby. My husband will kill you."

"I don't think so." He pulled out the black stone out of his jacket that Whitehead had earlier.

Immediately, the same twisting pain hit her gut. She hissed, trying to catch her breath. Her baby recoiled fluttered violently. "What...what is that stone?"

He examined it as if he were looking at for the first time. "It's a stone from your husband's home planet, Zalara."

"What..." she gasped.

"Why? Does it make you sick or ill? Interesting. Remember Superman? This is kryptonite to you, even your unborn child. If your husband comes, he's dead."

Gwen's heart stopped. "You bastard!"

He slipped the stone back into his pocket. "I wish things could be different, but it's either you or me."

Tears blinded her vision. She gritted her teeth. "I hope Theo burns you alive."

A silver knife glowed on an end table next to Donald's chair. "The priestess was right." He picked up the knife. "Apparently, we have unwanted visitors." He glowered. "Mason, get in here."

The door opened. Mason had a bandage on his neck, which made her smile.

But he didn't look at Elliott. He glared at Gwen with pure hatred. "What, boss?"

"Is there some kind of creature outside?"

He blinked. "What animal?"

Gwen sat taller in her chair and peered out the window. Whitehead was petting a bloodhound.

A jolt went through Gwen's body. She bit her lip to hide a

smile. Was it Martin? He was a shape-shifter and could transform into any shape. She could be wrong, but as far as she knew, there wasn't a bloodhound in Magic. Although someone could have gotten one.

"Any kind of animal..." He broke out into another harsh cough.

Mason jerked his thumb. "There's a bloodhound outside."

"That's not a dog, you fool. I told you–there's magical creatures here. That's a shape-shifter. Kill it."

Mason looked at Elliott as if he were crazy. "It's just a dog."

Magic was good about keeping her secrets, secret.

Elliott shoved the silver knife in Mason's face. "This means that thing is a shape-shifter. Kill it now."

Gwen squirmed and screamed. "Run, Mason!"

The bloodhound led out a howl.

"Shut up, bitch!" Mason backhanded her across the face.

Pain exploded in her mouth, snapping her head back. She cried out.

Gunfire stilled her heartbeat.

Whitehead raced back into the cabin. "Boss, Mason, I ain't never seen nothing like it. The dawg...he...just disappeared."

"That's because he's a shape-shifter, you fool," Elliott wheezed. "Thanks to you two idiots, they're coming."

Whitehead scratched the top of his greasy blond head. "What's comin'?"

Elliott stabbed the knife into the recliner. "A dragon." He flicked out his hand. "Go out and hunt that dog. You better damn hope you got it, and it's out there dying." He looked at Gwen. "Don't look too hopeful, my dear. Both these boys' guns have silver bullets and for what I'm told, just one nick of silver is enough to drop a full grown shifter."

Numbness gripped her chest and she hung her head. A tear slid down her cheek and splashed onto her thigh.

Please, God, don't let them hurt my husband or my baby.

CHAPTER 10

The sun had sunk and the full moon crescent was over the horizon, but Martin wasn't back yet. Both he and Leif had flown all over Magic and not one hint of Gwen. Theo looked at Cé and Leif and tilted his beer. "Are we clear on the plan?"

Cé took another swig of beer. "We've gone over it twelve times."

"Aye," Leif agreed. "Where is that damn dog anyway?"

A hummingbird darted toward them then descended onto the ground. Frantic wings turned into fast flapping arms and the bird grew six feet. The beak disappeared. Feathers turned into skin and hair.

Theo glared. "Martin, where the hell have you been?"

Martin ran his head through his brown hair. "That was damn close. The bastards were shooting silver bullets."

"Where are they?" Theo demanded.

"Up the road, a couple of miles away."

Theo and Leif glanced at each other then back at Martin.

"We've both been flying all over this place." Theo tipped his hat up. "How could we have missed it? I couldn't sense her at all."

"That's because Donald and his two idiots have set wards around the house." Martin grabbed a bottle of beer out of the cooler on the porch and took a big gulp. "The cabin's invisible."

Cé flinched. "You're kidding?"

Martin shook his head. "No, I'm not. One of them, I think it was Mason, opened the door that just came out of nowhere. I saw her Theo. She was there."

Theo's breath bottled up in his chest. He grabbed his shoulders. "How is she?"

Martin avoided his gaze.

His arms shook and his heart fluttered. Theo dug his fingers into his flesh. "Tell me. What did they do to her? Is she alive?" His voice turned into a growl and he pulled back his upper lip.

Martin hung his head. "Yes, but…"

"But…what?"

He sighed and slowly put his hand on Martin's shoulder. "I'm sorry, Theo. They beat her."

Theo tilted his head back, his dragon roared. "No!" Smoke spilled out of his nose.

A strong hand grabbed his arm. Leif glared. "Listen to me. Stay calm. Remember your damn plan."

Theo closed his eyes and took a deep breath. He thought of Gwen and her soft scent and touch and forced the rage back, but it was there…waiting to explode.

Cé slapped Theo on the back. "We need to stick to the plan."

"Aye," Leif agreed. "Martin, d'ye need to sit this one out?"

Martin wiped the sweat off his brow. "No, just give me a minute. I like Gwen. I don't like people coming to our town and torturing our folks. It's not right."

"According to Topper, we're the strongest at midnight, but I'm not waiting until then. Based on the dark magic, we could be killed." He studied each of their faces. "Are you with me?"

Cè tilted and raised his bottle. "I'm in."

Theo clanked his against the glass and smiled. Cé winked.

Leif followed suit. "Damn right." His golden eyes glowed and smoke swirled out of his nose. "They'll regret hurting my sisters."

"All for one." Martin transformed into a French Musketeer. He had a purple plume in his hat and a long red tabard with a white cross on his back. He lifted his bottle as if it were his sword strapped to his waist. "And one for all."

Leif frowned. "What the bloody hell are you supposed to be?"

Theo laughed and lowered his beer. "He's a French Musketeer."

Martin unleashed his sword and swished it in the air.

Cé smirked. "Do you even know how to use that?"

Martin wiped the sword underneath his throat, forcing his head back. "When I transform into a creature, any creature, I know all their skills. So, yes, I know how to use this." He narrowed his eyes. "Any more stupid questions?"

Cé put his hands up. "No. Remember, I'm on your side."

"I know." Martin sheathed his sword.

Theo raised his eyebrow. "Is that what you're going to go as–a Musketeer?"

Martin smiled. "I think I'll unnerve them. They'll be looking for an animal." He pulled out his police special. "But unlike the Musketeers, I have no intention of using their flintlocks." He studied his gun. "This is much more accurate." He replaced it into his holster then motioned with his arm. "Shall we?"

Leif frowned. "Can you find this place without being a dog?"

He smiled. "Absolutely. Once I get a scent, I never forget it."

"Let's go." Theo put his beer down on the small wooden table.

"Aye," Leif nodded.

Three other bottles joined Theo's. They looked at each other and then headed off the porch.

Martin pointed west. "It's about two miles from here off Skull Road."

"They'll be expecting us to fly or drive," Theo said. "We walk and take them by surprise." Their boots crunched on the pebbles. Each held a sword or a gun in his hands.

Theo's heart beat harder and his skin grew hotter as the dragon within him threatened to bulk out. God, what if when they got there, Gwen wasn't alive. She was his whole life. He should have put a tail on those two convicts.

Stupid. Stupid. Stupid.

The cords of muscle on the back of his neck tensed, and he gritted his teeth.

Stay calm.

When they had walked a couple of miles, he slowed his step and gasped for breath. He broke out in a hot sweat.

Leif clasped his arm. "Theo, what's wrong? You don't look good."

He shook his head. "I don't know. I feel like my energy's being drained. Maybe its the black magic Topper talked about." He wiped the perspiration off his forehead.

Martin, Cé, and Leif all looked at each other.

"I don't feel anything, Sheriff," Martin said.

Cé shook his head. "I don't either."

Neither of them were dragons. Theo eagerly looked at Leif.

Leif gripped his shoulder. "Sorry, Sheriff, I donna feel anything."

Theo frowned. "But you're a dragon. If I'm being drained, you should too."

Leif shrugged. "Sorry, but I'm not."

Theo glared at Martin. "Are we close?" He refused to admit if they kept going, his strength would run out. Something was really wrong.

Martin stopped and pointed. "There it is."

Theo frowned, trying to keep from releasing his rage, and lifted his arm. "All I see are cacti, pinyon pines, and scrub brush."

"It's there. I told you. It's invisible."

Cé looked at Martin. "Bloody hell, how are we supposed to carry out the plan if we can't see it?"

"The house is where a bunch of cacti are surrounding the rocks."

"Are you sure?" Leif asked.

Martin motioned. "Trust me. It's there."

Theo cleared his throat. "We all know our jobs."

Leif cleared his throat. "Are you sure you can do this, Theo? You donna look good."

A loud agonizing scream froze Theo's blood. "I'm fine. Are you with me or not?"

"Aye." Leif transformed into a dragon. He flew in back of the cacti.

Theo unleashed his beast. Wings thrust out of his back and a tail grew out of buttocks. He grew two sizes. His mouth and nose elongated. Smoke swirled out of his nose. The weariness melted away and strength flowed through him. Maybe it had only affected his human side. He flew into the front of the cacti and prayed that Martin wasn't mistaken.

Cé went to the west side of the cacti while Martin went to the east side.

Prickling rushed over his scales. Martin better be right about this, because his dragon fire could smite a dragon, a musketeer, and a vampire. The last thing he wanted to do was smite his friends. Theo took a deep breath and blew. Fire blazed onto the cacti. Suddenly, a revolver formed out of midair and fired. Pain slammed into his shoulder, piercing his hide. Blood drizzled down his leg. He screeched.

"Theo! Help us!" Gwen's desperate voice spurred him to move.

Suddenly Donald appeared out of thin air. He sneered. "Hello, Sheriff." He held a shiny black stone in his palm.

A tidal wave of weariness slammed into Theo and he winced, lowering his head. He lifted his head, but he couldn't budge—as if he had turned to stone.

"Interesting," Donald murmured. "This little stone turned you to stone."

"You bastard, what did you do to him?" Gwen yelled.

"If you'll excuse me, Sheriff, I must attend to your demanding mate."

Theo struggled, but his muscles stubbornly refused. He'd never felt anything. He was frozen in his own skin.

A loud crash that sounded like glass breaking broke his attention, but then his heart stopped. Cé screamed.

God, he couldn't let his friends die. He needed help.

He forced himself to concentrate, ignoring the moans and groans and screams.

Queen Cosima, hear me. I need you.

A vision formed in his mind.

"Theo, I hear you." She appeared in his mind, sitting in her chair. Her dark hair was piled up on high her head. Her yellow gown shimmered.

"Queen Cosima, I can't move."

"I know. It's the Nebulous Stone." Her eyes were filled with dread. Damon stood behind her, his face grim and his shield drawn.

"What is it?"

"The Nebulous Stone is from Zalara's core. It draws on our power."

"How the hell did it get to Earth?"

"Millions of years ago, Zalara had active volcanoes. One of them, Zeus, erupted. The fierce eruption nearly split Zalara in two. Zeus spewed lava and stone high into the air. Bits of the stone were hurled into space."

"How can that be? Stones would have been disintegrated in the atmosphere."

"Ordinary stones–yes," she said. *"But not the Nebulous Stone. It's powerful, and protects its self. The stones must have floated to Earth."*

A hard pounding echoed between his ears. He strained to lift his head, but he still couldn't move. "That's not possible."

She lifted an eyebrow. "Because you don't think it's possible?"

More cries from inside made his chest tighten.

"Just tell me what to do."

She didn't answer, and his pulse quickened.

"Queen Cosima, forgive me. I fear for my friends and wife. Please, please help me."

"Is the stone in front of you?"

"I don't think so. The bastard took it with him."

"Good. That gives you a fighting chance. Dragon fire burns in your heart. It's very powerful. Concentrate on your heart. Build the fire within you and crack the spell."

"How?" *he gritted his teeth.*

"You must pour all over your energy into your heart. I warn you that I could be dangerous."

A sour tasted formed in his mouth. "How dangerous?"

"It could kill you."

Her dead voice sank his stomach to the floor.

Gwen screamed. "Stay away from me."

"Please help me. Gwen's my life. She's my whole world."

"Concentrate, Theo."

He focused on his heart. Pouring all of his dragon power into his heart. Power increased through him, but when he moved, he could only lift one talon.

"Is it working?"

"I am trying."

"Listen to me. I will ask the Fates to help you. They are our goddesses and protects us from evil."

The Queen lifted her arms and cried out in a loud voice. "Fates of Zalara. Please hear me. Help Theo. He needs you."

Darkness swirled into the room, blocking out Damon's frowning face and everything except the queen. She was a burning light. Lightning flashed and crackled, then it sizzled toward Theo like a beam.

Adrenaline spiked through him. His heart sped faster than a Ferrari. His eyes flew open. He jerked his head up and his wings flapped, stirring dust into the air. He spewed fire as he burst into the cacti. More agony cut into him as if stalagmites were plowing into him, slowing his movement to a crawl, but he refused to give up.

"Leave him alone, you bastards!" Gwen screamed.

Another anguish released the rage inside him. He dragged his talons across the ground. The gravel turned into hardwood floor. He inhaled the scent of wood, ash, and fear.

He wasn't outside anymore. He was in a cabin.

Elliott stood smiling, holding the dreaded black stone and a blade underneath Gwen's chin. "Good evening, Sheriff. Take a step and she's dead." His skin was still ashen and he looked like something out of a concentration camp, but a triumphant glare flared in his eyes.

Theo growled, but remained perfect still. He'd no idea where Leif and Martin had gone.

Gwen looked at him with tears glistening in her eyes. She had a black eye and a purple bruise on the left side of her cheek.

Cé was slumped over in a corner with a blade in his heart.

"Your friend isn't doing so well. The blade has been dipped in a dead man's blood in a graveyard under a new moon. According to Madame Mthunzi, fatal to vampires."

Theo snarled. Cé was a good man. He didn't deserve this.

"You'll pay for interfering–*Impetus*."

Black smoke rose out of the stone and split in two. Half of it disappeared underneath a door next to the fireplace, while the other swirled up Theo's nose. Sweat drenched him. He struggled to breathe. Unbearable anguish swept through him as if fire ants were attacking him from the insides. Instead of freezing, he was burning as if he were melting. A puddle of sweat formed underneath him. How was this possible? He was a freaking dragon.

"Greetings from Madame Mthunzi. Those are her wards–lethal to a dragon."

"Stay away from me," a woman screamed from somewhere in the cabin. It had to be Grace.

Gwen's lower lip trembled and she stared at a door. Grace must be in there. God, who knew what was happening to her, but he was powerless to do anything. If he made a move, the bastard would slice Gwen's throat.

"What the hell are you?" a man yelled.

"Your worst nightmare–*Monsieur*."

A man screamed. The door next to the flickering fireplace opened and Whitehead staggered out. His hands were over his heart, his eyes wide. He wobbled and fell on his knees. Blood seeped through his fingers. "Mason?" His voice faded, and he fell onto his side.

"No!" He rushed over to Whitehead's motionless body. He shook his shoulders. "Shawn, Shawn, answer me."

Whitehead's listless eyes stared blindly.

"Get a hold of yourself," Elliott growled.

Mason glared. "He was my cousin, you bastard!"

Theo transformed back into a man at dragon speed. "Gwen." He gritted his teeth as blistering pain surged through him as if he were floating in lava.

"Theo, what are you doing?"

"I can't…fight him as a dragon. Pain. So much…pain."

"Yes, my dear," Elliott said. "The stone beat down a dragon. Any size dragon."

"But not a shape-shifter." Martin stood in the doorway, holding his blood drenched sword.

Elliott blinked. "What the hell are you?"

Martin raised his sword. "Isn't it obvious, *Monsieur*? I'm a Musketeer. One for all and all for one."

Mason slowly stood and reached for his revolver. "I'll kill you."

Before Martin could move, Mason fired. Silver bullets riddled him.

Martin slumped to the floor.

Mason kicked one of his legs. "That's what you get for killing my cousin."

Theo growled and took a step toward him, but he slipped on the puddle and crumpled to the floor.

Another loud snarl came from the bedroom. He pulled back on the trigger. "Another one of your friends is going to die."

Agony ate through Theo's palms and knees. Sweat poured down from his face onto the floor, and he panted hard. He stopped. Tightness spread across his chest. He was a powerful dragon and could do nothing to save his woman and his friends. What the hell was burning inside him?

An agonizing scream crushed Theo's hope that Leif had survived. Soreness welled up in the back of Theo's throat. The dragon within him roared and he fought to gain control he had to tell Gwen. She was their only hope.

"Gwen…listen…to me."

Elliott forced Gwen's head back with the knife. A trickle of blood dripped down her throat.

"You'll die soon, Sheriff," Elliott said. "The minute you passed the doorway, the stone attacked you. And I'll soon live forever."

Ignoring the pain twisting inside him, Theo stared at Gwen. "Queen Cosima said…draw on our baby's power. You have to call her. She has…the power…to change… the stone…to light. Only you…can do it. Trust me. I love you. I believe in you."

"What? What are you talking about? The stone won't let her release any powers."

"The baby's got…special…" He gritted his teeth and fell onto his side. Pain rolled up his arm and bore into his heart. Something was moving inside him, shredding his insides.

He opened his mouth, but spit out blood. God, he *was* dying.

CHAPTER 11

Gwen froze in her chair. Her breath stopped. Please not both him and Grace. Theo lay curled up in a ball and wasn't moving. He was her life. "Theo." Tears streamed down Gwen's face, but she was no shrinking violet.

"Sweet baby, help us. We need you," he whispered.

She could barely hear him. How could this be true? She didn't have any powers.

"Yes, sweet baby, help us," Elliott jeered. He wrapped his fingers in Gwen's hair. "I'm tired of waiting. Your baby can't hurt me. I have the Zalara stone. Your baby's as helpless as his useless father." He lifted the knife as if to cut her throat.

Gwen tilted her chin up. "It's not a him, you bastard. It's a her." Her belly stirred, growing stronger. Her heart pounded and tingles swept over her, making her hair stand up. Heat surged through her, but she wasn't sweating.

"Your skin..." Elliott's eyes widened. "It's turning red. What's happening?" He fumbled, putting his shaking hand into his pocket. He yanked out the stone and put it right in front of her face.

She didn't care. Her heart pounded faster, but it wasn't just hers. She could feel her baby's. Every time the baby's heartbeat, more and more power pulsed through her. Adrenaline flushed through her like an out of control forest fire.

Her nails elongated. She dug them into the chair, tearing the wood. She smiled. "You were saying?"

Elliott screamed and jerked his hand out of her hair that was on fire. He dropped the knife and stepped back. "What's happening?" He looked at the stone. "Why isn't this damn thing working?"

The restraints on Gwen sizzled up. Her body was on fire, but she wasn't burning. She walked toward Elliott. "My baby's very, very, very angry with you. You want her blood?" She picked up the knife and slashed her hand. "Take some."

"No! Please!" He palmed the stone and thrust it at her.

Something invisible slowed her step and her stomach cramped. She put her hand on her tummy. "We can do this, daughter."

Power slowly pumped through her, but then churned faster. She smiled. "Time's up, codfish." She knocked the stone out of his shaking hand, hard. The stone dropped to the floor. She snatched it up before he could. Fire sizzled her hand and she screamed.

"Gwen, no," Theo gasped.

"Help me, daughter," she whispered.

The stone burned in her hand. Her heart swelled and power pushed through her veins. Coolness rapidly rolled down her arm. White light burst between her fingers as if she gripped a star.

Elliott grabbed her fist, trying to pry open her fingers. "The stone is mine. Give it back to me."

"Do you really want it?" She slowly opened her eyes. Bright blue light flashed into room.

He shielded his eyes. "What have you done?"

"Ruined your plans." She smiled. "Your turn."

"No, no, stay away from me." He put his shaking hands up.

But Gwen ignored his pleas. He planned on drinking her blood and killing her baby. She didn't care that he was dying of cancer. Normally, she would have tried to help him, but he threatened her family.

She clutched his face with her bleeding palm, pressing the stone against his cheek. Elliott's face turned bright red. He beat at her wrist and kicked her, but she held on tightly. Surprisingly, she didn't feel a thing—as if a shield protected her. The stench of human skin made her choke. His arm dropped limply to his side. His face melted into goo and he screamed. His body turned into ash. She released him. His bones, and what was left of his flesh, collapsed onto the floor in a heap of dust.

Her skin slowly cooled and she caught her breath. She looked at the stone in her hand. It had changed from black to bright blue. Warmth filled her. The terror of the night fled.

She slipped the stone into her pocket, then hurried over to Theo. Tears spilled down her face. His skin was so ashen, and he was curled in a ball.

She took off his white cowboy hat and pushed back his thick hair, her hand shaking. "Theo, don't leave me."

"Gwen," he groaned.

"Theo." She pressed her palms on his rugged cheeks. "You're alive?" She kissed him again and again on his lips, needing to feel his breath mixing with hers.

"I guess so."

"Of course, he is," a familiar voice said.

Gwen looked up to see Topper standing in the doorway. "Topper, what happened?"

"You destroyed the evil, Gwen. The boys weakened the magic when they rushed the house, but your trust in yourself, and in Theo, allowed you to defeat the darkness."

Gwen frowned. "But I'm not magical. How can this be?"

"You are now, my dear. You mated with a dragon and the little one inside has made you powerful. Otherwise, you wouldn't have been able to change the stone from evil to good. Not only did you save Theo, but your friends as well." She pointed. "See look."

Gwen turned where Cé had fallen. Giddiness rushed over her. He pulled the blade out of his chest. "Bloody hell. I need to sleep for a week."

Theo stirred and Gwen helped him to sit.

"So, after the baby's born?"

"She'll still be magical." She winked. "I suggest you don't make her mad, Sheriff."

Theo glanced over at Elliott's steamy remains. "Yeah, I think you're right."

"You're telling me." Martin dusted his hat off and stood.

Gwen lifted her eyebrow. "So, let's not start now."

Theo put his hand on the back of her neck and kissed her. "I can't wait to get you home."

"Tell me." Cé scratched his head. "Are you still going to walk around like a musketeer?"

Martin shrugged. "Maybe."

Leif walked out of the bedroom, holding an unconscious Grace. Tears rolled down his face. "Gwen." He voice trailed off, and his Adam's apple moved up and down. "I think they raped her."

Grace shook her head. "No. Elliott said they wouldn't."

Theo put his arms around her trembling shoulders. "Elliott lied."

Martin sheathed his sword. "When I came through the room, Whitehead was on top of her, groping her, but he had his pants on."

"She was naked," Leif growled.

Martin hung his head. "I know. He paid for what he did to her."

"Aye, so did the other one." He kissed the top of Grace's forehead. "She's so delicate."

"She's stronger than you think," Topper said quietly. She

walked over to Grace and ran her wand across her forehead. A yellow beam formed across her forehead, but then faded. "I built a wall that will keep back some of the memories, but unfortunately, it's not permanent. She'll sleep."

"Leif, take her to my house."

He nodded.

Topper flipped her hand. "You need to get her out of here. In fact, I suggest you all leave this evil place. My coven and I must destroy the cabin, so it does not attract more darkness."

"You donna have to tell me choice," Cè murmured. "I'm ready to see Pandora."

"You'll have to wait," Topper said. "She's part of the coven."

"She's here?"

"Yes."

Cé sped across the room and went outside.

Theo clasped Gwen's hand. "Let's go."

Gwen nodded, but she couldn't speak. Her sister was hurt. If only she knew about her power earlier, maybe Grace wouldn't have been attacked. She was such a gentle soul.

Theo and Gwen quietly left the awful cabin. She gripped his hand tightly. When they got outside, women were chatting. Cé and his wife were kissing.

Leif transformed into a dragon and flew into the sky, his talons clutching Grace. Theo quickly changed and Gwen climbed up on his back. He flapped his wings and air rushed over Gwen. She pressed her legs against his side. She inhaled his campfire scent that always made her feel safe.

All she wanted to do was fall into Theo's arms, but she had to take care of Grace like she always had. Tonight was going to be a long night.

∽

"Gwen, Gwen..."

A soft voice penetrated Gwen's brain. She immediately woke. She couldn't believe she fell asleep.

Gwen opened her eyes.

Grace was propped up on the pillow, her face whiter than the sheets. She bit her lip. "Are you well? Is the baby..." Tears spilled down her bruised cheeks.

Gwen clasped her shaking hand. "Yes, I'm fine. So is the baby. The baby saved us, Grace." She put her hand over her fluttering tummy.

Grace frowned. "What do you mean?"

"Theo told me I had to ask for the baby's help. Our little one has powers and she transferred them to me." She squeezed her sister's fingers. "I turned Elliott into a fiery ash. They're all dead. They can't hurt you anymore."

Grace nodded. "I know. A musketeer..."

"Martin. He's a shape shifter and he likes to turn into crazy characters."

"The musketeer stabbed Whitehead who was on top of me. Whitehead said he was done waiting until midnight. He tore off all my clothes." She broke into sobs. "I couldn't stop him. I begged him to leave me alone. I wasn't strong enough."

Gwen grabbed some tissues and wiped her sister's wet cheeks. "You were tied up, Grace."

"I am so ashamed."

Gwen brushed her hair back. "You have nothing to be ashamed of. I wished I would have known about the baby's power before. Why didn't Topper tell me?"

As if on cue, Topper flashed into the room. Her hair was the color of a rainbow that she swirled into a beehive.

Grace gasped and gripped the covers tightly.

Topper sat on the edge of the bed. "The cabin is destroyed and the black magic will not be able to come in through that doorway." Her voice softened. "How are you feeling, my dear?"

Grace turned away. "Not well."

"Topper, why didn't you tell me about the baby's power? I could have stopped all of this from happening." Gwen couldn't hide the resentment in her voice.

"Obviously, because I didn't know. Your husband isn't always good about sharing."

"Tell me about it," she murmured. "I'll have to talk to him about his secretiveness."

"Since you've been pregnant, I have been doing research. I know about dragons, but not dragons from outer space. So, I visited Zalara where Theo came from." She held up her hand. "I spoke to the Queen, Cosima. She's the one who told me about the baby's potential powers. You see if it's a girl, girls do not change into dragons, but they possess other powers." She smiled. "As you can see. It was the queen who told me."

She patted Grace's arm. "I just wish I would have found out sooner. But by the time I did, you both had been taken, and a dark veil prevented me from finding you. Luckily, you had Theo and his posse."

Someone knocked softly on the door. "Gwen, Grace, can I come in?"

Grace knotted the blanket, but didn't answer. Her cheeks were bright red. Gwen squeezed her hand reassuringly. "Aye, Come on in, Leif."

Leif opened the door. He looked at Topper. "How did you get in here?"

Gwen frowned at his harsh voice. "Leif."

"No worries, hon." Topper shrugged. "I come and go as I please."

He clutched his sword, his knuckles turning white. "I see. Topper, you promised to send me back when this was over. I've got to get back to my wife, Isabella. I miss her."

Topper smiled. "And I will. I don't go back on my word. Whenever you're ready, I'll open the portal and send you back."

He relaxed his grip on his sword and smiled. "Good. I've got to get back to my wife, Isabella. 'Tis time to go, Grace."

Grace tilted her chin. "I'm not going back."

"What?" A vein flickered on Leif's cheek. "Do you think that's wise? Look what happened here. You'd be safer with Morgana Fey. She wouldn't have let this happen."

Topper narrowed her eyes. "Let this happen? Is that what you think we did?"

Gwen glared. "Donna take that tone, dear brother. I can recall awful things happening to Isabella, to Mariah, and to Hannah. Hannah was almost raped as I recall."

Grace winced.

"Sorry," Gwen muttered. "But here. She doesna have to worry about a demon hunting her down." She folded her arms across her chest. "Can you guarantee nothing will happen to her back in our time?"

Leif opened his mouth and shut it. He rubbed the back of his neck. "No, I canna."

"'Tis Grace's choice," Gwen said, softening her voice. "You'll be at sea with the rest of the pirates and Grace will be at Morgana's, but she's getting old. I fear her time is near. Then, what will happen?"

He turned his head and he clenched his fists. He took a deep breath. "You'll come find me if you're both in trouble again?"

Gwen glanced at Topper who smiled.

"Of course. Besides, Theo, Martin, Cé, and a coven of witches are here to protect us." She patted her belly. "And one fierce little baby."

The tensed muscles on Leif's face relaxed and he smiled. "My nephew is quite the fighter."

"Niece," Gwen corrected.

He shook his head. "Still willing to argue with me?"

"Always." She got up and hugged him tightly. "I'll miss you, dear brother."

"And I, you." He released her and walked over to Grace who had tears in her eyes.

"I'm so…"

He put his finger on her lips. "You fought bravely, little sister. Even restrained, you fought. I'm proud of you. If you want me to come back, tell Topper and I'll come." He kissed her fingers. "Promise me?"

"I will. Tell the others I love them. I'll return someday. I just canna face them yet."

He kissed the top of her forehead. "You have friends there. Hannah, Isabella, and Angelica, know what you've been through. They were all kidnapped and almost raped, too."

Tears glistened in her eyes. "I know. When I'm ready, I'll come."

"Good-bye, little sister." He stood. "I'm ready."

Topper motioned with her hand. "Then, come with me, dragon. I need to summon the coven. We'll send you back today." She clasped Leif's arm and then they both disappeared.

Grace burst into tears. Gwen rushed to her side.

"If you want to go home, I'll summon Topper."

"No, I'm not ready. Leif will tell them what happened. How can I face them again?"

She clutched Grace's hand and squeezed it hard. "Because you're strong, Grace. All of those women have faced perils like you, and come out stronger."

Grace pushed her hair behind her ears. "But they all have powers…I donna. I'm just human."

"Women have experienced this for years and have survived. You will, too."

Grace bit her lower lip. "I donna what I did without you."

"We're twins, Grace. I need you as much as you need me, especially with a dragon baby on the way."

"Can I stay with you? Will Theo mind?"

"Of course, not," a male voice said.

Theo held his hat in the doorway—his broad shoulders nearly the width of the door.

Gwen hurried over and hugged him. He held her. His thumping heart sent reassurance through her.

"Grace, our home is your home. You stay here as long as you like."

Gwen looked up at him. "I love you."

"And you have my heart."

CHAPTER 12

Six months later

Theo sat at his computer at work, typing in his last traffic ticket. Frost was less than pleased he'd gotten a ticket, but driving his space ship down Main Street was not allowed. It's engines melted Cé's brand new motorcycle, and the two almost came to blows.

He took a sip of coffee. He liked being in the office alone. Martin was out doing patrol and this gave him time to get things done without Martin's constant changing into different forms.

Topper flashed into his office and Theo jumped, spilling his coffee on his lap. "Damn it, Topper. Look…"

"Hush," she said. Her hair was white and her face grave. "You need to come with me immediately."

He stood and grabbed his car keys. "Why? What's wrong?"

"It's Gwen. She's gone into labor."

His heart skipped twenty beats. "But…"

Topper grabbed his hand. "We don't have time to lose."

In a flash, Theo tumbled through space as if he were on a roller coaster.

They both landed in Theo's living room. Against his better judgment, Gwen had wanted to deliver the baby at home. Her sister, Grace, was a mid-wife, and she trusted her more than she would any other doctor.

A loud scream stilled his heart. "Gwen!"

Topper snatched his arm. "Theo, wait."

"What?" He yanked his arm free.

"You need to be prepared." Her voice hit him like a torpedo, hitting all of his worst fears.

"What?"

"The baby's breached. She won't turn."

"Then, we have to get Gwen to hospital." He whipped out his phone to call 911.

Another cry made him tremble.

"Gwen doesn't want to go. She believes in her sister."

"I don't care what she thinks."

Topper lowered her voice. "Listen to me. It's important that Grace does this."

He glared. "You want me to put my wife and baby at risk, so Gwen's sister can feel good about herself?"

"You don't understand, Theo. Your baby would never let anything happen to her mother or her. You must trust her."

Gwen cried out again. He was done arguing with Topper and rushed down the hall to his bedroom. He burst through the room. He was too stunned to move.

Gwen was pressed up against pillows on the headboard. Her fists were balled up into the sheets. A blanket covered her from the waist up. Her legs were spread apart, her knees bent. Blood pooled around her.

Her sister, Grace, had her hand inside, Gwen. "Donna push, Gwen. I have to turn her."

Sweat poured down Gwen's face and she gasped breath. "'Tis

hard." She glanced over at Theo and stretched out her hand. "Theo!"

He rushed to her side. "We've got to get you to the hospital."

"NO!" She thrust her head back and squeezed his hand hard.

Pain crippled his fingers, and he gritted his teeth.

"I've almost got her," Grace said. "Come on, sweetheart, turn for your auntie."

Gwen squeezed Theo's hand tighter and tilted her head back.

"Why didn't you call me?" Theo pushed her damp hair off her face with the blanket. His throat constricted. He wished he could do something to help her.

She licked her lips. "The...contractions...came so fast. I called...Topper." She leaned her head back and panted.

"Grace...I feel another contraction." She tightened Theo's hand.

He clamped his jaw tight. His insides quivered. God, he wished he could take her pain.

"Donna push. Not yet."

Moaning, Gwen dug her nails into Theo's palm, and he hissed.

"She's turned!" Grace sat back and pulled her hand out of Gwen. "Now, you can push."

Gwen screamed and tossed her head back.

"Theo! Look, I can see the crown of your daughter."

"Go!" Gwen ordered, as she released his hand.

He stood next to Grace and his mouth dropped. His heartbeat raced and time stopped. His daughter was edging out of Gwen's vagina. His baby!

"One more time, Gwen," Grace said.

Gwen yelled. Her face turned bright red, veins pulsing on her temples. Any minute, Theo thought she would explode. He didn't know what to do.

His daughter slipped out into Grace's hands. She released a healthy cry and bright light bathed the room as if a ray of sunshine dropped from the sky.

Grace cut the umbilical cord and handed Theo the baby. He smiled. He loved Gwen with his whole heart, but this little girl opened up the flood-gates of his heart.

He looked at his daughter and then his panting wife. He knelt next to her and kissed her forehead. "Look at what we did."

Gwen opened her shaking arms and he handed over his daughter. "She's beautiful. What should we name her?"

"Sunshine," he said. "Sunshine."

Grace wiped her forehead. "'Tis a beautiful name."

Tears glistened in Gwen's eyes. "Thank you, Grace. I couldna have done this with you." She looked up at Theo. "I want her middle name to be Grace."

He smiled. "I wouldn't have it any other way."

CHAPTER 13

One month later

Gwen moaned as a delightfully warm pulse of pleasure rippled down the length of her body and back again. She opened her eyes with a soft sigh and gazed up at the tanned, naked man laying next to her and wondered if the grin he wore was a threat or a challenge.

Since her kidnapping, she wasn't the same woman. Her powers had gotten stronger and she delighted in knowing she could set things on fire if she wanted, which always sent her handsome sheriff frowning.

"Good morning," he said.

"Morning." She stretched her arms over her head and yawned. "What time is it?"

"A little before six."

He ran his hand down her naked flesh and she shivered.

"I see you're in an amorous mood." She lowered her voice. "Sunshine's asleep for now."

Her daughter touched her like no one else ever had. Between her and Theo, she counted herself as being blessed.

He smiled. "How can I not be when I'm next to such a beautiful woman?"

She clasped his wondering hand and kissed his knuckles. "I love you."

"I know." He slid his other hand up her hips to her waist to her breasts, stroking his slick fingers around one breast, circling and brushing the nipple until it budded. She caught her breath, trying to remember what the hell they were talking about.

"Would you like to prove it?"

"Aye, please, Theo. Before your daughter awakens."

He laughed and rolled on top of her. He moved his hot mouth down her throat to her other breast. He lavished it like until she was gasping. She cradled his head to her breast and arched her back, allowing him to take more of her flesh into his mouth.

"Always." She gasped and looked nervously at the door, wondering about her sister. Grace was getting stronger, especially after helping deliver Sunshine, but often times, she wanted to be alone. Sunshine was the one who could always make her smile. She truly was sunshine to Grace's darkness. "Is Grace still asleep?"

"I'm sure. She doesn't get up until around seven anyways, and I have to be at work by seven thirty." He inserted his finger between her curls, stroking her and stirring an aching passion.

She panted. "Let's...start your day with something...to remember me...by."

"Yes, let's do." He parted her legs and pressed his hips between hers. His stiff cock pushed against her soft folds.

He kissed her, branding her as his. She clutched his shoulders and returned his fervor. He slid his cock deep into her core. His eyes were wide and gold and filled with the vision of how he loved her and believed in her. He proved his belief in her time and time again.

He rocked his hips and she wrapped her strong legs around him, pinning him. Their rhythm was slow then glided into a steady and then hard pace. Gwen shuddered as an orgasm filled inside her, taking her higher and higher. Her rapid heartbeat matched his. Blood gushed through, ending at her core.

Theo's eyes glowed darker, meaning he was approaching his own ecstasy.

She clung to him and arched her back as fiery bliss rolled over her. She cried out his name.

He pounded harder and harder against her until he thrust his head back and growled, spilling his seed deep inside her.

"I never...never." He panted. "Get tired of hearing you call my name."

She threaded her fingers through his hair. "And you, my fiery dragon, chase away my darkness."

He kissed her again. She didn't know what was in store in Magic, since everyday brought surprises, but she knew for sure that Theo would always be there–her dragon in shining armor.

~

Did you love reading about Theo and Gwen again in **Touch of Darkness**? Do you want to find out more about the Fates of Zalara? Check out the Dragon of Zalara series. Sign up for the Supernatural Scroll and you'll get the last news about my books!

Find out what happens next in Magic.

The next book in the series is The Touch of the Dragon and this is about their baby girl all grown up!!! Her biggest and most dangerous task is to protect dragon eggs!

But she's got loads of trouble because Madame Mthunzi is up to her old tricks, but this time, there's a new villain and he's more powerful and evil than Donald!!!

Excerpt from The Touch of the Dragon~

Chapter One

"Please, don't kill me." Madame Mthunzi's lower lip trembled and terror mirrored in her huge dark eyes. Her bright yellow, orange, and black dhuku slid off her head, revealing curly black hair.

Rhain almost felt sorry for her.

Almost.

"Tell me where the time amulet is, Madame Mthunzi. I'm tired of your games." Rhain's dad, Ian, pressed the dagger deeper against her throat. The light from the flickering candles glistened off his jeweled rings. He narrowed his golden eyes. "If you value your life at all, you will cease this charade."

"Dad." Rhain grabbed his dad's wrist. "Slicing her throat isn't going to help us find the amulet." He cast his gaze over his dad's impeccable clothes. He curled his lips up into a sneer. "And you'll get your prized Gucci suit dirty."

"I don't care. I'll buy a new one. Unlike you, I care about my appearance."

Rhain shrugged. "Wearing a monkey suit isn't my style."

His dad jerked his wrist free. Black hair fell across his dad's thundering face. "I don't like extortion." He dusted off his jacket sleeve where Rhain had touched him as if he had cooties.

His dad's obsessions and stinginess was enough to drive a saint mad. Rhain should have walked away years ago, but Ian was all Rhain had after his mother and sister were murdered.

"I wasn't…I wasn't extorting money from you." Madame Mthunzi's voice shook.

Rhain folded his arms over his broad chest, stretching his black T-shirt. "Actually, you were. You wanted us to give you fifty thousand dollars." Strobe lights annoyingly blinked around them as if they were supposed to be lightning. Skulls and creepy candles littered the shelves. "I suspect these little dramatic quips you have and paintings of ghosts and demons in here are designed to milk or scare clients. I doubt you even possess any magic."

Madame Mthunzi shook her head. "That's not true." She stuck out her chest. "I am a voodoo priestess."

Rhain rolled his eyes and stuffed his hands into the back of his jeans. "Is that supposed to impress me?"

"Yes, it is." But he could still hear the tremor of fear in her voice.

Rhain gritted his teeth. "Well, Madame Mthunzi, we tracked the amulet to you."

Her eyes widened. "I don't know anything about an amulet, I swear."

Rhain narrowed his eyes. "I would suggest you refresh your memory. My sources tell me that you sent a Donald Elliott to a secret location that had a dragon baby."

She frowned. Recognition flashed in her eyes. "Did you say dragons?"

"Yes." His dad tapped her temple with his finger. "By the light in your eyes, I take it your small brain remembers this?"

She gripped the armrest of her Queen Anne chair, digging her long red nails into the leather. "What does a dragon baby have to do with an amulet?"

His father traced the blade down her heaving chest. "*That* is not your concern."

Madame Mthunzi's lower lip trembled. "But...Donald...died... five years ago."

His dad tipped her chin back with the blade. "And?"

She licked her quivering lip. "I sent...him...to Magic, New Mexico."

Rhain took his hands out of his back pockets. He rubbed his stubble chin that he'd forgotten to shave for the last couple of days. "Magic, New Mexico? I have heard whispers of this place, but I never thought it existed."

"Oh, it exists. Magic's an enchanted town that protects the supernatural. I sent...I sent Donald there because he was dying. If he drank a baby dragon's blood, he'd be cured."

Bitterness ran down Rhain's throat into his tight gut. All mercy he had for the terrified woman vanished. He stared at a shelf. "I bet she's got baby dragon bones in those jars. Slit her damn throat."

Crocodile tears ran down her ruby cheeks. "No, no, I swear. I don't."

His father smiled–a smile that would stop a demon in its tracks. "Not yet. She still hasn't told me what I want to know."

More tears leaked down Madame Mthunzi's pale face. "Please, don't kill me. I can take...I can take you there." Her voice cracked and the whites of her eyes were huge.

Rhain didn't trust her. Based on what he'd learned of the woman, she'd conned old or dying people out of their life savings.

His dad carefully slid the blade in a special made pocket in his jacket.

Rhain swore under his breath and flicked his hand. "You're not actually going to trust this charlatan, are you?"

"I want that amulet." He grabbed Madame Mthunzi's arm and hauled her out of her chair. He shook her hard. "Don't even think of betraying me."

"I won't." Her puny voice only irritated Rhain further.

Rhain ran his hand through his long hair. "Seriously? We just have the Toyota truck that you insisted on driving."

"My Escalade is too conspicuous. Anyone that knows me will recognize her. No one will suspect us in the truck."

Rhain bit back another retort. The damn Toyota was cramped as it was with him and his father. With Madame Mthunzi between them, Rhain wouldn't be able to breathe.

Madame Mthunzi looked wildly around the room stuffed with her supposed magical skulls, candles, and masks. "I need to get some things."

"Do I look like a fool, Madame?" His dad pulled her close to his side. "You'll not bring anything that's magical."

She pushed on his hand. "Why not?"

He released her abruptly and she stumbled into her table, knocking her crystal ball off its stand. She lunged and grasped the ball, just as it reached the edge of the table.

"Because I refuse to have either my son or myself be cursed like you've done with so many of your victims."

She gingerly put the crystal ball back on its stand. "You don't understand. I can't go into Magic without being armed."

Rhain lifted an eyebrow. "Unarmed?"

She rubbed her arms. "Yes. One of the witches banished me from ever stepping into Magic again. If I cross over the barrier, I'll die."

Ian combed his thick black hair. "Interesting." He flashed her a hard gaze. "Why?"

She straightened her shirt and stuffed her hair back under the bright colored dhuku. "Because I might have cast an evil spell."

Rhain hooked his thumbs into his belt loops to keep from strangling her. "This is getting better and better. What the hell do you mean by might?"

She stopped fooling with her hair and dropped her arms. "The head of the witch's council, Topper, wouldn't allow me to come into their coven, because she said that I had cast a spell over some of the inhabitants."

"Imagined that," Rhain growled. "And?"

She straightened her shoulders. "Well, they were all rich and didn't need all of their money. They could spare some change. I was down on my luck and needed the cash."

Rhain gave her a cold stare. "Based on what I've discovered about you, you're always down on your luck."

"Enough of this." Ian threw up his hands. "We need to leave for Magic now."

Rhain's stomach growled in protest. He rubbed the bridge

between his nose. "Dad, we've been driving for over eight hours—without anything to eat I might add. I need a break. Magic isn't going anywhere."

His dad reached into his jacket and pulled out the truck's keys out of another hidden pocket. "No, the town's not. But the amulet could. You don't know what ends the Fates will do to protect the amulet."

He handed the keys to Rhain who shook his head and backed away.

"Fine." Rhain held up his palms. "But you're driving. And we're not leaving until we at least go through a drive threw."

His father glared. "I can't believe you're thinking about food when we're so close."

"You mean you're so close. You're the one obsessed with the amulet. You just dragged me along for the ride and to be your body guard."

Out of the corner of his eyes, Rhain saw Madame Mthunzi stuff something into her skirt pocket.

He grabbed her wrist and pinched hard. "What are you hiding?"

"Nothing." Her innocent voice only set off the frustration bursting inside him.

"Do you want me to shake you upside down until your teeth rattle?" He slammed her against the wall. "Show me what you put in your damn pocket."

He wasn't dumb enough to reach into her pockets and pull out what she was trying to hide. He'd learned the hard way about touching magical objects.

His father pulled back his upper lip, revealing sharp teeth. He looked he was about to shift and scare the skin off Madame Mthunzi.

She reached her hands into her pockets and pulled out two smooth stones–one green, the other brown. On closer inspection, they were hand-carved skulls.

"They are my lucky skulls. I take them everywhere with me. Please, don't make me leave them."

Tears glistened in her eyes and she held the stones to her chest, no doubt attempting to gain some sympathy. "Please."

His father scowled. "Hold out your palms."

She slowly did as he asked. He ran his hands over the stones. "I don't feel any magical vibrations, Rhain. I think she's telling the truth. They're just worthless stones."

Madame Mthunzi's pupils dilated, and she cast her gaze to the right.

"Dad, she's lying."

His dad gestured with his hand. "Feel it for yourself."

"Fine I will."

Rhain ran his hand over the stones, never taking his eyes off Madame Mthunzi. Just like his dad, he didn't feel the slightest tremor.

"Feel anything?" His dad's annoyed voice made him shrink with frustration.

After hunting with his father for the past ten years, he'd developed the ability to sense magical objects. Usually tingles would run up his arm, but with these stones, he'd felt nothing.

Something was wrong. He knew she was lying. Maybe she was more powerful than he thought. Powerful enough to hide her magic from dragons.

Rhain stood straighter. "No."

His dad jammed his finger into Rhain's chest. "Never doubt me again."

A flicker of smugness glinted in Madame Mthunzi's eyes that sent chills down Rhain's back.

His dad slid in front of the madame and motioned. "Let's move. I want to get to Magic before morning."

Madame Mthunzi flashed him a ha-ha smile as she followed his father out of her dark room into her house of masks and voodoo dolls.

He glared at her back, clenching and unclenching his fists.

Bringing this voodoo priestess to Magic was a bad, bad, bad idea.

Unlike his father, he wasn't convinced that the stones weren't magical. She was hiding something—something that sent shivers down to his toes.

DEAR READER

I hope you liked a *Touch of Darkness*. This book was originally a kindle world book under Magic, New Mexico. I fell in love with Theo and wanted to continue with his story. In Touch of Madness, you found out where he came from, but I wasn't done yet. He was such a delightful character that I had to continue his story.

If you loved the characters, you can read more about them in the Madness Unleashed, which is my Dragon of Zalara series. It has witches, aliens, and of course, dragons. You'll find out more about Queen Cosima and her guard, Damon.

Would you like to find about freebies? Sign up for my newsletter, ML Guida's Supernatural Scroll, and you'll receive the first books in my other series.

Also sign up for my private Facebook group, ML Guida's Supernatural Lounge, for exclusive giveaways and sneak peeks of future books. I hugely appreciate you spreading the word about *Touch of Darkness*, including telling a friend.

I'm off to write the next book! Join me on my newsletter or Facebook group.

DEAR READER

Farewell for now,
ML Guida

ABOUT THE AUTHOR

Award Winning Author M.L. Guida loves the paranormal. Even when she was four years old, she would watch the soap opera, Dark Shadows, and fell in love with vampires! Who wouldn't want a bite on the neck? But she didn't stop there. Witches, dragons, angels, and demons are sprinkled throughout her books.

Today, she continues to love the preternatural and watches Supernatural, Paranormal Survivor, and A Haunting. Like Dean Winchester, she loves to write alpha males who aren't afraid to face the forces of evil.

ALSO BY ML GUIDA

Dragons of Zalara Series

Madness Unleashed

Madness Unhinged

Madness Unmasked

Madness Unbalanced

Bears of Aria (Scifi Romance)

Walfea

Vaughn

Tash

Magic New Mexico

Touch of Madness

Touch of Darkness

The Touch of the Dragon

Touch of Curiosity

Other books in Magic

Blood Brotherhood Series

Sin of the Vampire

Shadows of the Vampire

Heart of the Vampire

Mate of the Vampire

Claim of the Vampire

Destiny of the Vampire

Bite of the Vampire

Blood Brotherhood Box Set (Vol 1- 4)

Stand Alone

Dark Promise

Angels of Death Series

Betrayal

Deception

Punishment

Cupid